WHATEVER YOU ARE IS BEAUTIFUL

Richard Blandford

Spencer Macleavy Press

As always
for Emily and Ella

PROLOGUE

Not so long ago, I was sat on the side of a bridge, my legs dangling down. Beneath, a river flowed many times faster, it seemed, than the rush hour traffic behind. Next to me was a man in a silver bodysuit. Its reflective sequins caught the sunset, a rainbow of colours rippling across his body.

The man's name was Bo, but he had lately taken to calling himself The Trout.

I explained to him that what had happened between me and his wife was a mistake and meant nothing, and my interests currently lay elsewhere, with people of his own kind.

Bo did not seem to hear me. Perhaps the traffic was just too loud. Or perhaps he didn't want to. Or perhaps it was because he was wearing a heavy moulded plastic helmet that resembled the full head of a trout.

Within minutes, both of us would have fallen from the side of that bridge. This is the story of how we got there, and what happened next.

STAGE I

HEROS AT HOME

When I first met Bo, he was not The Trout. He did not wear a trout helmet and costume. He had no troutlike tendencies at all, as far as anybody was aware. In fact, there had been only one meaningful incident with trout in his life at that point. He was just an ordinary man, it seemed, living an ordinary life with his wife, Paynter, and his two small children, Mason and Skiff. They had a small house on the outskirts of the medium-sized, relatively affluent, town of Merriweather. His job in construction did not leave them financially comfortable, but at least they were stable. But Merriweather was not ordinary, and neither was Bo. Not anymore. Merriweather was one of several HEROS hotspots in the North-Eastern states of the US, and Bo had it.

Since the first appearance of HEROS (Heterogenous Enhanced Replacement Organ Syndrome) in a few isolated individuals a decade ago, the condition had fascinated and baffled the medical community in equal measure, as it had the world at large. With the sudden emergence of case clusters, or 'hotspots', in the past year, it felt as if we were perhaps entering a new, unsettling era.

lips sinking, following the contour of his drooping moustache, as if he were a child pulling a sad face. The sound got that bit louder, and I felt a tiny pain behind my eyes. A glass tinkled in a cabinet.

And then it stopped.

'Well,' said Bo, letting go of the table top. 'That's it!'

'That's it?' I said. Did I sound sarcastic? However hard I tried to be sincere, a little drop of sarcasm always came out. Too many years of practice. Now it was ingrained.

'That's it. Something just happens in my throat and I make that really low noise, and…'

'And what does it do, that noise?' I asked him. Again, the sarcasm. Why couldn't I lose it? It was a curse.

'Not a whole lot,' said Bo, laughing. I nodded, empathically, as I listened to the reply. That's what I wanted to be known for now, instead of the sneer. An empathic nod. 'It's just that noise… sometimes it gives people a headache. As you heard, sometimes it'll rattle a glass or something. But it hasn't ever done any damage, as far as I know about, anyway.'

'Tell him about the trout, Bo,' said Paynter, laughing, from a corner of the room where it was too dark for her to turn up on camera well.

'Oh, yeah, the trout! I did it near the river once…'

'…and the trout jumped right out!' Paynter finished his anecdote for him.

'Yeah, onto the bank. Must have been ten of them.

I guess they were spawning. You wouldn't believe fish could throw themselves like that. Just lying there, flipping about. We had to throw them back in the water. Crazy.'

'Maybe that's really your thing,' I said. 'The ability to control trout.'

'Well, maybe, Chad. Maybe you're right.'

'What you going to do with a power like that?' said Paynter, brightly. We all laughed. It was then I noticed how joyful the sound of her voice was.

***

Two days earlier, I had been lying in bed back home with my partner, Sam. That evening she had cooked one of the several Sri Lankan dishes she had learned to make in childhood ridiculously well, while I packed. After watching some old *Seinfeld*s, we'd had going away sex, and then, as we lay there, she'd said, 'Hey, how about you stay here with me instead of going to silly America?'

She didn't mean it, obviously. She had accepted at last the explanation that only long-term residents of a hotspot ran the risk of catching it. And besides, I had to go. Everything depended on me going. No one had said anything. Not anyone from the channel. Not my producer Jolyon. But there was a feeling in the air. A creeping sense of boredom from all sides. A boredom with me.

People had been bored of me before. I'd started out catching the tail end of the new lad movement.

My programmes were freak shows. Has-been celebrities on the comeback trail, eighty-year-olds losing their virginity, a Loch Ness Monster-worshipping death cult, all of that. Comfort food for the people at home, telling them they were normal — it was these guys who were crazy! And all delivered with a barely concealed sneer that the interviewees never seemed to catch but the audience always did. But that was over. People finally got tired with my schtick. And I was more bored and disgusted with it than anybody. Had been since Season Two. Not that it stopped me doing Seasons Three to Nine. But it did send me into a cocaine spiral that lasted a near-decade, making me almost as famous for my using as my programmes. The industry in-joke was my nickname was the same as my actual name. And as far as the press and the public were concerned, I was as big a prick offscreen as on.

By Season Ten, after the big crash and rehab, I reinvented myself, not just because I was getting called out on social media for being 'problematic', but because I literally could not make another programme like the old ones, prodding vulnerable people with a stick for laughs. Now I was seeking to empathise with the strange people I talked to, make them human, even when their weirdness had taken them to dark places. I was caring. I even cried on camera once. Some critics didn't buy it. Said it was a cynical turnaround. But they didn't know. They didn't know what it was like to drop the sarcasm, the irony, and say something and mean it. To stop looking for the skewer and give a natural human reaction to people in pain. After years of hiding in plain sight, the only thing I cared about now was being true.

And it paid off. The public liked the new me, for a little bit. But Season Ten's ratings were down on the year before. It shouldn't have mattered. The channel, which I was better than but evidently not so much better I could easily go to another one, filled its schedules with bad US imports and reality TV, but had an obligation to make the occasional doc to keep their licence, however low they scored in the ratings. And yet, there were younger faces coming through to do them, with new perspectives, fresher styles, and who could attract that lovely advertising revenue that bit more easily than I could. Worse, I was coming to the end of my contract. They hadn't said they weren't going to renew, but why would they? What I did didn't cost that much, but the new kids on the block, farmed over on YouTube, could do it cheaper and from their bedrooms. I'd already reached out, seeing if there might be any interest in me doing a podcast or even a bit of radio work. And there were some who would be happy to have me, as long as I came cheap. So that's where I was heading. Not out, but a lower profile. Low enough to be labelled a has-been. A blow that even my post-coke ego would struggle to handle. Unless I turned it around this time. Unless I really delivered.

I'd made a programme about HEROS when the first cases appeared. It was way back in my sneering phase, so I made fun of the costumes and their silly names, pretended that I wanted to be like them and dressed up with a cape and a mask and my underpants outside my trousers. Jolyon had been on at me to return to the subject for several years as the story got bigger, but I had always said no. It would be a step backwards, I said, exactly the sort of thing we were trying to get away from. But when the hotspots appeared, I saw that this was perfect. It was about communities now, families. And now that it was a recognised condition we could go for the medical angle too. It was so obviously the shot in the arm my career needed. But I had to be fast. Hotspots were giving the HEROS story a second wind, and it was getting bigger than Asperger's and white-collar psychopaths put together. If I didn't get my doc on by Christmas, someone else would make a HEROS House reality show or something and that would be it. And besides, me saving my career wasn't the only reason to do it. It gave me the chance to tidy up a mess I'd made. Back in the old days, I'd got people to laugh at HEROS. Now I could get them to care about it.

Still, lying in the bed with Sam, nearly half of me wanted to stay and never leave the flat again. I used to long to head to the US for filming. There was something about the iconography — the suburban houses with their little fences, the fast food joints, the healthy-looking girls with big smiles —

that made me think of the Hollywood movies I'd watched growing up about kids with pet aliens living in their lunch boxes, before shit got real and I was snorting more than I was eating. I never stopped half-thinking that Heaven would be an American kitchen with a big fridge.

The other half of me thought that Heaven would be Sam, forever. And if I played my cards right, that's what I would get, at least until I died of old age and forever ran out. It seemed like we were in it for the long haul, even though we never quite said it. She had been my publicist, dragging me round radio and daytime TV studios for interviews, just before I fell apart. Then, when I was alone in the flat unable to leave and the phone wasn't ringing, it was her who got in touch. And it was her who got me into rehab, and into it again when I relapsed. Even though she must have looked at me and seen a sad wreck back then, she must have also seen there was someone worth looking out for. Now I'd much rather be with her than at the Groucho or anywhere. Not that I go anywhere there's cocaine, and my friendship circle has been shrunk to those who don't take it, so pretty much no one.

Sam had been the final nail in the coffin of the old Charlie, and midwife to the new. Incredibly, I'd been faithful to her since Day One. A big thing for me. Up until then I'd been a serial monogamist. Or at least I would have been if I hadn't also been a serial cheater. But those days were far behind me now. I barely even connected to that cynical,

charming bastard, now I had my morning affirmations and occasional yoga. They say you're always
an addict, but with Sam in my life, I didn't feel
the urge for either of my old indulgences, save for
the very occasional pang. It was like a childhood
hobby I'd outgrown. Without the coke to give me
absurd levels of confidence, I was awkward around
women who weren't Sam. It would be difficult to
believe I was ever anyone different.

I buried my head in her tummy and kissed her
belly button, the black hairs that led downwards
tickling my nose. 'I want to stay,' I whimpered.
'Please, mummy, please let me stay.' Since I'd become the new mature me, Sam was the only one
I could be childish with. Sometimes I'd just make
a crude, laddish joke. Other times, like now, I'd almost be a baby. She was like my mum in a way,
even though she was nearly six years younger
than me. To tell the truth, although I could always
be relied on to go out and do my job, I'd never
been that great with the housework, or cooking,
or keeping myself in underwear without holes. I
think Sam wanted kids a bit. She'd made noises,
but she never pressed the issue, despite the ticking
of the biological clock. Sometimes it felt like she
was waiting for me to develop somehow, as if she
didn't think I was ready yet. Or, more likely, she
still didn't absolutely trust me not to relapse. And
did I even want kids? The idea of my life moving
forward made me nervous. Everything was in perfect balance, as long as Sam didn't expect me to be

any more of a grown-up than I currently was.

'So, stay,' she was saying, in that bed, in that room, which was like a giant womb for this man-child, setting me up to deliver my inevitable, adult response.

'I can't,' I said, as I rolled myself off the bed in the direction of the shower.

***

Three years ago, Bo coughed up his larynx. A new one had grown in its place and forced it out. It was identical to the one he had lost, except that it gave him the ability to make that peculiar sound and accompanying vibration he demonstrated in the kitchen. At first, he couldn't control it, he told me. He would feel it rising up from his throat and his face would contort as he struggled to contain what felt like a chainsaw revving up inside him. After a while, however, he found that he could force it down again. He eventually got so comfortable with the sound that he learnt to trigger it at will. Now it was almost a party trick for friends, although the children were bored with it already.

Bo had Stage I HEROS. No one knew if he would go on to develop Stage II or even Stage III. The odds were in his favour, but not by much. Some of the earliest cases of HEROS had still not progressed beyond the first stage, and so there was much hope this would also be the case for Bo. Still, his optimism seemed to me to be bordering on denial. I would have to tread carefully.

***

'Hey! Touchdown!'

Bo cheered as he let his young son Mason run past him and dive to the ground, placing the ball over a line in the back yard only they could see.

It was a sweet family scene, but I couldn't help feeling that Bo was trying a bit too hard to convince me that HEROS made no impact on his life at all.

Paynter called Mason inside, perhaps sensing I needed to ask Bo some difficult questions that were not for his ears. The sky darkened also, as if aware that a change in mood was required.

'Do you ever worry…' I began to say.

'No, I don't worry about nothing,' he said, cutting me off.

'No, but really,' I said, 'do you not think about what will happen to you and your family if you ever progress to Stage II and…'

'I'm not going to progress to Stage II because I'm going to make damn sure I don't. Just going to hold it back with sheer willpower, if I ever see it coming.'

'You didn't see Stage I coming,' I said.

'No, but I didn't know about it then. Know your enemy, that's how you win.'

'You see HEROS as your enemy?'

'Not really,' he said, looking slightly rattled for

the first time since I got there. 'It's just a... an inconvenience, like a flat tire or something. Actually, a flat tire is more of an inconvenience because you've got to change it. I ain't going to change nothing with HEROS. Just shut it down if it gets too big for its boots!' The life returned to his face. He had regained control of his own narrative again, after my attempts to wobble it out from his hands.

The cloud drifted past the sun on cue and Bo had his brightness back again.

'How about that Scotch, eh?' he said cheerily, slapping my back at the memory.

***

Paynter was standing in the kitchen, peeling hardboiled eggs. Glancing at their fridge as I stepped back inside, I saw that it was pleasingly large, although a collection of patriotic fridge magnets made me wonder where they stood politically. But I didn't want to think about that. I wanted to like these people.

'Hi, Paynter,' I said softly, not wanting Bo to hear me from the garden, where he was playing racquetball with Mason and Skiff. The racquets had to be fetched from the tool shed, and from the spiderwebs and detritus covering them, obviously hadn't been used since at least last summer. I left Laura filming them while I tracked down Paynter. It was her turn to become part of the story.

She looked up at me from her egg-peeling and smiled. It was a small but warm smile, as American as the smell of their breakfast. I realised I had been so busy with Bo, I had not really seen her. Strawberry blonde, as they said over here. Heavy freckles. Earnest eyes. She looked like the sort of girl I'd imagined my first girlfriend would be like growing up, rather than the pasty, slightly ill-looking English girls I eventually did go out with.

'Oh, hi, Chad,' she said.

'It's Chas, actually. No. Actually, it's Charlie. Not that it matters.'

'Oh, I just called you that because Bo does. You should correct him.'

'Oh, I have, but I don't want to press.'

'You really should correct him. Bo needs correcting sometimes!' She laughed.

'Is that your job?'

'You bet!' She laughed some more. I waited for the smile to fade naturally before I asked her.

'Listen, Paynter. You said it was OK when Laura was up here a while back to talk to you on camera. Is it still OK?'

'Uh, yeah, I guess. But I don't know what I'd talk to you about. I mean, it's all about Bo, isn't it?'

'No, not really. The documentary is called "Living With HEROS". It's about those who have the condition, but it's also about the people they share their lives with.'

'Oh, OK,' she said, blankly, as if trying to find the relevant file in her brain for the information I was giving her. I carried on.

'So I just want to ask you about how you feel about it. How it affects your life. What it's like for the kids. That sort of thing.'

She didn't say anything at all. Just looked at me with those eyes, gazing out through a sea of freckles, trying to work out what sort of creature I was.

'Well,' she said, finally, 'it doesn't really affect me all that much. Except that—'

'If you could just hold that thought,' I said. 'And tell it to the camera.'

***

As Laura drove away, I took over the filming and got a shot of the whole family waving goodbye to us from out front, just after we faked the arrival shot with Bo shaking my hand again. I looked at their house one last time with its cladding, the slightly faded Stars and Stripes flying from the porch, the 4x4 in the drive, and a front yard that led onto the road with no pavement in-between, and once it had disappeared from view, house after house, all looking pretty much the same, and in-haled it. You could see why so few of the residents of Merriweather wanted to move, despite the risk of HEROS. It really was a beautiful place.

To keep the budget down, we'd only hired one car, so wherever I went, Laura did too. Ok, she was the chauffeur. She was a much better driver than me, anyway. I could barely remember to keep to the other side of the road.

'So, Chas...' said Laura, 'What do you think we got?'

'Not much,' I sighed.

'We got our Happy Place,' she said.

'Yeah, but it's a bit too happy. There's no grit to it. Unless... do you think Bo's got a drink problem? It *was* quite early for Scotch.'

'Nah. I checked their cabinet. Quite high-class brands for a low-income family. He's a connoisseur, not a drunk.'

'And Paynter seems as healthy and chirpy as can be. No one's going to want to watch that for more than two minutes.'

I knew Laura agreed. Once the camera was on her, Paynter had never followed up on her 'except', however much empathic nodding I did to encourage her. She was in line with Bo now, perhaps because he was now in the room. HEROS was not a problem. After the initial shock of Bo puking up his own larynx and making strange noises, it barely made a dent in their lives. They were just a normal family. And no, she was not worried about Stage II. Bo would head it off as soon as it raised its head. She would help, if he needed her to, although she was sure he wouldn't. Her earnest eyes annoyed me then, because I thought they were hiding the truth, or at least I wanted them to be, for the sake of the programme. We would make a follow-up visit at the end of shooting. Maybe I'd get something then.

We'd got a few padding shots of yet more sports in the yard, Bo rocking out to Aerosmith, Mason's bedroom with Spider-Man wallpaper. It was enough for me to answer the loaded email from Jolyon that was waiting for me on my smartphone, asking if we'd done 'Great Things'. Yes, I typed back, we had done Great Things. But reading that, Jolyon would know that I knew that Great Things were not enough. Great Things just meant quality footage that would get a slightly positive review in a broadsheet. We needed 'Magic Moments', instances where it all just explodes and something extraordinary happens, and everyone talks about it for a week. This programme would need to be packed with them if it was going to save my career, but I was losing faith I could get any from Bo.

'Hey, I got a good feeling about this,' said Laura as she drove us onto the highway, back to the reasonably-priced hotel on we were staying in the other side of Merriweather, over the bridge that crossed the gushing Bradley River. 'This is just Day One. Day Two will be better.'

'Really?' I said, trying to hide my doubt.

'Really,' said Laura.

'You had a good feeling that time we went to film that hermit.'

'That went really well.'

'He nearly killed me with an axe!'

'It made very good TV.'

'Yeah, you're right. It did.'

Laura was always right. This would work.

***

After we ate in the kind of classic US diner I loved so much, and I was excited to find still existed in Merriweather, Laura headed for the hotel bar. Even in my party animal past, I could never outdrink Laura. She would be improbably bright of eye and bushy of tail tomorrow morning, like always. Not only was I still jet-lagged, meanwhile, but I was middle-aged, somehow much more so than Laura, despite her seniority. Even on an easy day's filming like today, I would now reach a point in the evening where no further activity was possible. Parts of me ached and everything suddenly seemed hard. I went back to my room.

I wanted to talk to Sam. It was now way past midnight back home. It would be selfish of me to ring her now, I thought, with her early starts. But still I rang her, and she wasn't annoyed, as I knew she wouldn't be. She was bleary but pleased to hear my voice. Not as much as I was to hear hers, but I wasn't keeping her alive.

We talked for twenty minutes, about the filming, mostly. I told her my worries until they weren't worries any more. And we said we loved each other and meant it. Afterwards I lay on the bed, still, giddy from tiredness and basking in the afterglow of the phone call. Everything is all right, I thought, in the moments before sleep, and laughed at how crazy that still sounded.

HEROS RIGHTS

'I mean, just look at this,' said Alex, as the packet of raisins slipped through her hands onto the floor of the supermarket. They did not slip through her fingers. The packet had passed through her hands which, for a moment, had ceased to be solid objects.

'This is why,' she continued, 'when people are like, you don't have a disability, you have a superpower, I'm just...' She fails to finish her sentence, seemingly lost in the injustice of it all.

Alex is in her early twenties. She wears combat trousers and jacket, her neon dyed hair in a pixie cut, and piercings in her nose and eyebrow. Three years ago, when she was in her freshman year of college, Alex awoke to the horror of a pair of hands next to her in her blood-soaked bed. They appeared to be her own, despite her having an identical pair attached to her arms. By this point, awareness of HEROS was such that Alex knew exactly what had happened to her. The only thing for her to do was to wait to see what strange ability her newly grown replacement hands gave her.

She did not have to wait long. While carrying

a tray in a dining hall, it fell to the floor, seemingly by accident. Alex offered to help the cleaning staff clear up the mess. However much she tried to grasp at the roll of paper towels, she could not tear one off. Her fingers would just slip through them. After a while, she apologised to the cleaner and gave up. Five minutes later, her replacement lunch dropped to the floor. At this point, she ran, crying. But she could not get out of the dining hall. Her hands slipped through the door she was trying to push open. Alex does not remember this, but she has been told she simply stood by the door, screaming, until someone called security.

Alex dropped out of college soon after, struggling to adjust to her condition. Like Bo, she had since learned to control what some would call her 'power', despite her dismissal of the term. It still caused her stress, however, as the amount of concentration needed to keep it in check was high, and she could not always manage it. Still, she struck me as having a steely determination to live her life on her own terms, despite the obstacles she had to overcome, not just those caused by HEROS itself, but society's attitude to people like her. My own attitudes were, it seemed, not helping.

In the supermarket, unthinkingly, I had reached down to pick up the bag of raisins.

'No, don't,' she said, sharply. 'I got this.'

Alex bent down, and concentrating hard, willed her hands solid enough to pick up the bag and place in her basket.

'I seem to have upset you,' I said.

She shrugged. 'Yeah, I guess,' she said.

'Why though?' I asked.

She said nothing. I repeated my question, sensing there was something she really wanted to say about what I had just done.

'You didn't ask,' she said.

'I didn't ask if...'

'You didn't ask if I needed help. You just saw me drop the thing, and went, OK, there's someone who can't do anything for themselves. I'll just take over, with my big, strong masculine hands that things don't fall through like they're made of wet tissue paper and then everything will be OK.'

I wasn't sure if she was right or not. Had I thought that? Or was it just a natural reaction, something I would have done for anyone, 'wet tissue paper hands' or not?

'I'm sorry if I upset you,' I say.

'Sorry *that* you upset me,' she says. 'You did upset me, so it's not a matter of *if*.'

I couldn't help feeling that Alex was being a bit oversensitive. But perhaps that was because of my privilege as a person whose hands did not turn intangible at inopportune moments.

We approached the counter. Alex started to unload the contents of her basket on the conveyor.

'I... I could do with a little help here, Charlie,' she said, as a bottle of sweet chili sauce refused to leave the basket.

'No problem,' I said.

'Oh, it's a problem,' she said. 'It's all a fucking problem.'

***

Alex was living in a hostel in downtown Merriweather for people with Stage I HEROS. She allowed me to see her room. It was little bigger than a prison cell, albeit one decorated with various HEROS Rights posters. 'WE'RE NOT YOUR $&! %ING HEROES!' read one. 'PHYSIOTYPICAL PRIVILEGE IS YOUR SUPERPOWER' said another. There was a bed, a desk and chair, some bags of clothes, and little else.

'Your room is quite bare,' I said.

'No point having things if you can't hold them,' she said.

'Really?' I said, getting a bit tired of what I was growingly perceiving as Alex's self-pity. 'I mean, I know this isn't the ideal living space, but you're obviously an intelligent person and I don't even see any books or magazines in here.'

'Yeah, you try reading a book when you can't turn the pages,' she said. 'Anyway, like everyone else these days, Mr. Gen X gonna-make-you-a-mixtape, I got this.' She pulled a phone, held inside a builder's chunky protective cover, out of her rucksack. 'I read on this. I watch TV on this. I listen to music on this. I talk to people on this. When the HEROS kicks in, I can let it drop and it'll just bounce. This phone is my room, pretty much.'

'Anyway, I gotta get ready for the demo, so...' she said, and headed back to her room.

***

'Here, I got a job for you,' said Alex, handing me a large placard and a thick marker pen. Can you colour in the letters? I'm not so good with pens.'

The placard read 'SOMEWHERE THERE'S A SPACE FOR US'.

'OK, I'll try not to mess it up,' I said, filling in the letters Alex had sketched out in pencil.

'Yeah, if you did, it would be pretty much a hate crime,' she said. 'Joking.'

Alex and other Stage I HEROSic residents of Merriweather were planning to march on the town hall and disrupt a local council meeting that evening.

'What is this demonstration all about?' I asked, trying very hard to keep neatly within the line.

'It's about creating a safe and adapted space for rosies in the downtown area. So, shops, social areas, facilities, all designed to be accessible and easy to use for us. We've been asking nicely for some time and got nowhere. So now we're going to ask less nicely.'

'But is that a realistic demand? I mean, to adapt an entire area of the town for the needs of a small minority—'

'Excuse me?' Alex cut me off. 'A small minority? Do you know how many people in Merriweather have HEROS? Four percent! We're a hotspot, Charlie! Did you not research this?'

I realised I'd made Alex quite angry. Perhaps this was partly my intention. I'd been playing devil's advocate so long, I no longer realised I was doing it. But I also wanted to understand her. I liked her spirit, yet I couldn't quite work out if she was a clear-headed activist righting serious wrongs or just someone with a chip on their shoulder demanding the world mould itself around them.

'I did my research,' I said, 'but all I'm asking is, is what you want tenable? I mean, HEROS manifests itself in so many different ways. You can't expect local government and businesses to pre-empt every single one of those. It's just not possible, surely?'

'Possible? It's amazing what's possible when people with power decide it's possible,' Alex snapped at me. 'Did you know there's a hotspot in New Zealand where it is illegal not to make provisions for rosies on commercial premises? You *meet* the needs of the community. You got a hotspot, you know there will be some sparkers like Janvier, some sandhands like me...'

'Sandhands?' I laughed.

'Yeah, sandhands. But that's our word. You can't use it.'

'Right.'

'Joking.'

I laughed. She didn't. She was on a roll.

'So you have fireproof park benches. You have

shopping assistant drones. You take down old phone wires for the gliders. A lot of it's basic stuff. The solutions are out there.'

I let her words hang in the air for a moment.

'I didn't mean to make you mad,' I said.

'You didn't make me mad,' she said, breathing deeply and calmer already. 'I just... I get tired doing other people's thinking for them. It's not my job to educate you, you know?'

I felt another tiny provocation creeping up and I couldn't resist.

'Well,' I said, 'it kind of is your job in this moment to educate me and the viewers at home if you want to win us over to your point of view. Without giving us the facts to support it, there's no reason for us to be swayed by your argument.'

'Oh, fuck off, Charlie,' she said, throwing a cushion at my head.

'Ow!' I cried out, although obviously it didn't hurt. Even though I was half-expecting it, it was jarring to see someone so articulate lose it so quickly.

'You really are a Grade A asshole, you know that?' She picked up the cushion and hit me with it. It hurt a surprising amount, for a cushion.

'A lot of your debating technique seems to involve insulting me and hitting me with a cushion. Not a complaint, just an observation.'

Still, I laughed, and I could see her laughing too. Finally, she stopped hitting me.

'You made me go outside the line, Alex,' I said,

pointing where my pen had squiggled right across her sign.

'Aggh! You're driving me crazy, Charlie!' she cried as she hit me again with the cushion, her fingers staying resolutely solid as she did so. I didn't mind. I knew it wasn't me that wound her up particularly. It was the world around her for which she was once made, but no longer was.

***

Alex's phone rang. She left it, waiting for it to go to voicemail.

'It's just my mom,' she said. 'It can wait.'

'Don't ignore it on our account,' I said.

'Oh, I'm not. It's... complicated.'

'Families often are,' I said.

'Yeah, not like mine.' Alex laughed nervously, and the call went to voicemail.

'Hi, it's Mom,' said a wholesome sounding voice. 'Just to let you know your father and I would love to have you over dinner this weekend. Give us a call. Love you. It's Mom.'

We sat in silence as the message lingered in the air.

'What was complicated about that?' I asked. 'Sounded like a really nice family scenario of you going over to visit your parents for dinner.'

'What's complicated, Charlie,' said Alex, deleting the message, 'is that my brother will be there.'

'Do you and your brother not get on?'

'You could say that,' she said. The nervous laugh again.

'Why is that?'

Alex psyched herself up to explain.

'My brother believes... my brother, he's a few years older than me, and he's a domineering asshole, so we've never been that close, but anyway, he's pretty religious. Very religious, actually. Mom and Dad are too, but my brother takes it... so far. He actually started going to another church when he was a teenager because the one Mom and Dad go to, I dunno, it didn't make you feel guilty enough about sex, which he's really into. The guilt, not the sex. Anyway, keeps on changing churches because he's always looking for something more hardcore, and the one he's ended up at now, the preacher there believes that people like me are... a punishment.'

'A punishment?'

'Yeah, because of all the homosexuality and porn in America, basically. They think God made HEROS to teach us all a lesson, and our enhanced organs, like my hands... they're made from pure sin. Like I literally have sin for hands.'

'You have sin for hands.'

'Yeah, it's crazy.' The nervous laugh. 'And because of that, my brother won't come near me, he won't touch me, he won't eat with cutlery I've held...'

'Will he even be in the same room as you?'

'Yeah, but he's always by the door, so if I move towards him, he can back out.'

'That sounds awful. And what do your parents think of this?'

'Well, they don't believe it, but… they respect it. Well, they have to. He's a fucking bully. They're scared of him, both of them. I mean, he's a scary guy. You'd be scared of him, no offence. Can you believe this? My mom has special cutlery for me because of him.'

'You're kidding.'

'I'm totally not kidding. I didn't know about it at first, and then I realised when my brother's children helped to clear the table and he gave them one of his looks that he does and they took everything except my things, and I saw, they weren't from the same cutlery set! She'd bought them specially. And then… this is the craziest part. Last time I was there, he made me wear gloves.'

'Gloves?' I couldn't help laughing.

'Yeah, like thin cotton ones you use if you're handling a sculpture or something. Said I had to wear them when I was at Mom and Dad's house. And I was like, no way, but Mom and Dad, they… they went along with it, like they always do, said that maybe it was for the best, just in case. And I was like, in case of what? And they didn't have an answer to that, but Jim was going on and on about it, and his Midwich Cuckoo kids were just staring at me like I was some monster from space the way they always do, and his wife was standing there with her stupid smile and it was all driving me so crazy that in the end, I was like, fine, I'll wear your damn gloves if that's what I have to do to see my own mother and father... So anyway, Mom and Dad respect his stupid, bigoted ideas more than they respect me and who I am, so, that's what hurts, and I can't get through to them what the problem is because he's the golden boy with the blond wife and the blond children he had super-young, and when they're all together, it's just a wall of God, and that's why I'm not picking up the phone and dancing down the street to go and have dinner with them.'

I had a thought. I wasn't sure if it was a good thought or a bad one. The idea oscillated in my mind between seeming truthful and cheap. What I did know was Laura had just had it too. She stopped filming.

'What if we came with you?' I said, softening my voice. 'Could we film you with your family?'

'Fuck off! No!' She sounded angry again, but she laughed when she swore. I knew that meant we could make it happen.

'Do they live near? Could we go there now? We've got a few hours.'

'Why would I want to do that, Charlie?' she said. 'What would it achieve?'

'Well,' I said, knowing in that moment that the idea was cheap and not truthful, and feeling sick from the unstoppable bullshit rising up within me, 'maybe if we're there it might give you a chance for you to communicate how you feel to your parents a bit easier? Obviously, we're not here to take sides, we're here to document, but if you know there's someone from the outside world there to witness it... I mean, it's just a thought.'

Alex paced. 'Oh my god, Charlie, you're such an asshole. I mean, how can you come out with such obvious crap? I know what you're trying to do, you manipulative prick.'

She paced. I said nothing. She stopped for a moment and muttered. She paced again. She came to a halt and faced me.

'But you know what?' she said. 'I'm going to give you what you want. How about that? The bullcrap reason for making me do something so dumb that you just pulled out of your ass actually has something to it. If Mom and Dad have to explain themselves to someone outside the family, they might see how insane it all is. And you'll get some good material for your sick, exploitative TV show and everyone's a winner! Oh, you're good, Charlie. You're a real professional. Professional asshole. But yeah, you're good...'

She picked up her phone. I nodded to Laura and she started filming again.

'Hi, Mom? It's Alex. Yeah, I'm good. Listen, are you and Dad free right now?'

***

We drove Alex, who like many HEROSic people is no longer allowed to drive herself, over to the suburb of Merriweather where her parents lived.

Along the way, she talked some more about how HEROS had affected her life.

'So you don't have a job...' I asked her.

Alex shook her head.

'Don't you think I haven't applied for stuff, Charlie. I'm always filling in forms, or getting someone else to fill them in for me when the pen won't stay in my hand. But whatever you do, it's wrong. If you tell them straight out you're a rosie, then you never hear back. Ever. Or if you hold out until the interview, and your hands start passing through things, which they always do because I'm nervous and I can't control it when I'm nervous, then they get mad at you for trying to hide it and then you still don't get the job.'

'What sort of work are you applying for?'

'Waitressing, mostly,' she said, her punchline landing right on the beat. I crack up, and so does Laura.

'Have you ever considered stand-up comedy?' I ask.

'Have you ever considered sit the fuck down and shut up?'

'I am sitting down, Alex. So that one didn't work so well. But well done for trying.'

'Is your show just you flying round the world being an asshole to people?'

'It used to be. So, I'm guessing you receive benefits?'

'I get SSDI now.'

'That's Social Security Disability payments.'

'Correct. But do you know how hard it is for most rosies to get that? And you know why?'

'Why?'

'Because in the first instance they don't see it as a disability. They see it as making you somehow better, with gifts that make you even more employable. Like we're all going to be working in the lumber industry or something. You have to prove that your "enhancement",' Alex actually finger-quoted this, 'has no value whatsoever in any workplace before you get the money.'

'And how did you do that?'

'I dropped a shitload of stuff on the floor at the assessment.'

'Deliberately?'

'No, of course not. Just accidentally enough to make a point.'

'You have a boyfriend?'

'Creepy question, old man.'

'Yeah, but do you though?'

'Nah.'

'Why not?'

'Partly because I just don't have room in my life for a man in my life right now, with organising the protests and just concentrating on getting through day by day. And partly because my girlfriend wouldn't like it.'

'You have a girlfriend?'

'Kinda. But it's really casual. Like, she'll go with other people sometimes, and I don't.' The nervous laugh was back.

'Sounds amazing. Does she have HEROS too?'

'No. She's an ally, though. She'll be at the demo later.'

'Where do you see yourself in ten years' time?'

'That's a stupid question, Charlie.'

'I'm sorry. Does it make you think about Stage II?' She glared at me.

'What do you think?' she said. 'Anyway, I don't see myself anywhere in ten years' time because all I'm thinking about right now is ways to make next month, or next year, more bearable for us.'

'I admire your focus and dedication.'

I thought she was going to reply with sarcasm, but all she said was 'thanks'.

***

We pulled up onto the drive of Alex's parents' house. It was much larger than Bo's little bungalow. Because of her hardened attitude to life, I'd imagined Alex coming from the American working class too, but now I saw that her background was much more affluent.   A curtain twitched in the front bay window as we stepped out of the car.

'Oh, where do your parents stand on the, you know, girlfriend thing,' I whispered. 'Do they know?'

'Yeah, they know,' she said. 'They think I'm going to Hell but it's OK for me to come to dinner as long as I leave my girl at home and wear a dress.'

'I can't imagine you in a dress.'

'I have some nice dresses. They're kinda stitched together from other dresses, but I like 'em.'

'You make them yourself?'

'Yeah. That surprise you?'

'Kind of. I didn't have you down for a seamstress.'

'Because of my hands?'

'No. Because you're... you.'

'I'm full of surprises, Charlie.'

'I noticed.'

'Yeah, well. Anyway, maybe I don't sew so much anymore.'

She looked sad at the thought of yet another loss, there on the driveway of her parents' house. I didn't know what to do so kept on walking.

The door opened before we could ring the bell. A grey-haired man in a burgundy V-neck sweater stood inside. He looked nervous.

'Hey, Dad,' said Alex. He nodded, but said nothing.

'Hi, I'm Charlie,' I said, offering my hand. He shook it, weakly, as if he was suspicious of what it might do.

'Yes, Alexandra said about you on the phone,' he said, in a voice as thin as paper. 'I'm Michael, Alexandra's father. You filming now?'

'Yes, is that a problem?'

'No, it's not a problem,' he said. I was unconvinced.

I asked if he wanted us to take our shoes off and he said yes. He led us into the lounge with the bay window. What struck me was how needlessly big everything was. The ceiling was high, the three-piece suite was overly plump and the television was even bigger than mine, and I was an overgrown child with money. There was a real, unlit fire with a mantlepiece that reminded me of a proscenium arch in the theatre, and mirrored sliding doors that made the room seem twice as large. We all seemed dwarfed by it all, especially Michael and the small woman who waited for us inside.

'Hi, Mom,' said Alex, giving her mother a hug that seemed to surprise her.

'Hello, Alexandra,' said the woman, as if summoning courage from deep inside her just to speak. 'Now, I just want you to know—'

'What's going on, Alex?' A man's voice, and not that of Alex's father.

'Oh my god, oh my god,' said Alex, with her head in her hands. 'How could you do this to me, Mom? I said I didn't want him here and I just wanted to talk to the two of you.'

'Your father felt it would be better if Jim were here,' said her mother, whose name I would later learn was Kathryn, 'so you didn't get too carried away in front of the camera, because you do get carried away and say some quite unnecessarily harsh things about your father and I sometimes...'

'Someone has to be here to stop you running your mouth off and lying, Alex,' said a youngish red-faced man with Nordic features, including the most piercing blue eyes, not noticeably shared by the rest of the family, stepping through the sliding doors. He was almost absurdly tall, much of the extra length in the legs, making him the only person there who was in proportion to the room. Wearing a shirt and tie as if he had just stepped out of an office, he seemed to be vibrating at a different frequency to everyone around him, filling the air with an angry tension that even the most aggressive people I'd encountered usually had to build up to. That no one responded to this except for a slight flinch suggested that they had grown used to his behaviour over the years, however unsettling it appeared to an outsider.

'Where are the gloves I gave you?' he said.

'I'm not wearing the gloves, Jim,' said Alex.

'You know the rules. You want to come here, see Mom and Dad, you wear the gloves. Now, where are they?'

'I haven't brought them with me, obviously.'

'Yeah, because you didn't think I'd be here, so you went back on our agreement. Can never trust you, Alex. Fortunately, I brought spares.'

Jim pulled out a pair of white cotton gloves from his back pocket.

'Put these on,' he said, dangling them from high up above Alex.

'I'm not wearing gloves.'

'Put on the gloves or you're gone, and your friends are gone, and I'll have a restraining order taken out against you so you don't get to come round here no more.'

'You can't have a restraining order taken out against me because I won't wear gloves, you maniac!'

'You'd be surprised what I can do, Alex.'

'It's best if you put on the gloves, Alexandra,' said her father. 'For the time being. Until we can… I don't know. Maybe there's a better way.'

'There is no better way,' said Jim. 'Put on the gloves. Now.'

Finally, Alex sighed with resignation.

'Fine. I'll put on the damn gloves. One last time. And then the gloves are over.'

'We'll see,' said Jim, dropping them down for Alex to catch.

'Hi, I'm Charlie,' I said, stepping forward, offering my hand. 'And you are…'

'Hasn't Alex told you all about me? I'm her evil brother, Jim.' He didn't shake my hand.

'I have heard something about you,' I said, 'but I'd be keen to hear your side of the story.'

He looked me up and down. 'Yeah, I bet you would. Like you wouldn't chop it up and change it to make me look bad.'

'I really am just trying to document Alex's situation, which you're part of. I promise I'll represent your point of view fairly.'

'Well, we'll see, won't we?' he said, puffing his chest out as far as he could with his parents in the room. 'I'll talk to you, but if I don't like what you do, I'll set my lawyers on you. And they always win.'

'You won't have to do that.'

'We'll see,' he said, quietly, before snapping his fingers and raising his voice back up to a level that reverberated off the ornaments. 'Right, let's get this kangaroo court started. What are your questions?'

'Well, actually, I'd rather like to start off talking to Alex's parents, if that's OK…'

'No. I'm the family representative. You're not going to talk to them. You're going to talk to me, and that's it. And then you leave.'

'You do know that we're filming now, so this what you're doing now could end up as part of the documentary?'

'I don't care,' he said. 'Your viewers can hate me as much as they want. All I'm interested in is me and my family don't get misrepresented. Which is what will happen if you let Alex shoot her mouth off.'

I resented Jim's attempt to dictate the terms of our filming, and was taken aback by the intensity of his personality. The fact that Alex, normally so outspoken, had now fallen silent with her head down wearing the hated gloves told me much about the dominant role Jim played in the family. But I had to keep the situation rolling, and so I offered a compromise that would in some way flatter Jim's sense of his own importance.

'What if we talked to you first, and if you're happy with the line of questioning, then we can ask your mum and dad some questions?'

Jim considered for a moment.

'Fine. But the chances of you getting past me are nil. Just so you know that.'

I nodded that I understood. This wasn't going to be easy, I thought, but it was probably going to be interesting.

***

I suggested to Jim we go outside where the light was better. He said we should do it here in the lounge. I asked him why. He said just because, and I sank into one of the armchairs and felt it swallow me up. I leaned forward the best I could. Jim banished his parents to the dining room beyond the sliding doors, telling them they could come out if and when he said so. He sat in the middle of the enormous sofa like some suburban emperor. Alex sat in a chair well away from Jim, pulling at the fingers of her gloves. I'd persuaded Jim to let her stay in order to give her right of reply, on the condition that she be made to leave if she got too uppity.

'So, what you got, Charlie?' said Jim, an unfriendly smile on his lips. 'Give it your best. Come on, hit me.'

I didn't say anything. I hoped it would seem as if I was building up anticipation. But sitting there, faced with a religious nut whose every motivation was to be found in the Bible, it occurred to me I had no idea what to ask him. I hadn't prepared for this interview. I didn't even know I was going to do it when I got here. But now I could see the only way to getting to understand his position was through his faith. The problem was I knew nothing about it. True, I'd attended a CofE boarding school, but I'd absorbed practically none of the religious stuff they taught us, save for the Christmas story and maybe half the Easter one, and what little I had taken onboard I'd let slip out my brain the moment I got my GCSE results. I knew there were Protestants and Catholics and an old half and a new, but what was Jim and did he just read one bit or another or both?

The silence went on. Now it was too long, and clear it wasn't intentional. Jim raised his eyebrows and did an impatient dance with his head. I just had to say something. Say anything.

'The Bible,' I said, with a little too much gravitas for what followed. 'Um, what's the best bit?'

Jim shot me an appalled look.

'The best bit? What's the best bit of the Bible?'

'Er, yes. What's the best…' I dribbled off into nothing. I'd interviewed some intense people before, but there was just something about his near-unblinking blue gaze that undid me. Even though we were sat at the same level, he somehow still managed to loom above, as I struggled not to sink in the puffed-up armchair that seemed to want to eat me alive.

'You mean Testament?' he was saying, contemptuously. 'Book? Chapter? Verse? What?'

'Verse!' I cried. They were the short things, I remembered now. 'Yes, what's the best verse?'

Jim shook his head.

'For Pete's sake, Charlie,' he said. 'Having faith in Jesus Christ isn't about having a favourite part. You take all of it, from start to finish, no questions asked.'

'Well, maybe not the best bit then, but your favourite. The part that makes you most happy when you read it.'

He sighed. 'Well, like I told you, it doesn't work like that. But if you really want to hear something good and true, which a snake like you is going to need before the time comes, how about this?'

And then he began reciting from memory, fixing me with a fierce blue-eyed gaze as he did so.

'For I was hungry, and you gave Me something to eat. I was thirsty, and you gave Me something to drink. I was a stranger, and you invited me in. Naked, and you clothed me. I was sick, and you visited me. I was in prison, and you came to Me. Then the righteous will answer him, Lord, when did we see You hungry, and feed You, or thirsty, and give You something to drink? And when did we see You a stranger, and invite You in, or naked, and clothe You? When did we see You sick, or in prison, and come to You? The King will answer, and say to them, Truly I say to you, to the extent that you did it to one of these brothers of Mine, even the least of them, you did it to Me. Matthew 25. Verses 35 to 40.'

There was a respectful silence. Jim looked

pleased with his oratory skills.

'Thanks, Jim, that was beautiful,' was all I could say, finally.

'The words are beautiful,' he said, 'because they are true. Now, Charlie from England, can you tell me what they meant?'

I was not prepared for this. I had only even been half listening, trying to think of a way out of this conversational dead end I'd led us down. I frantic-ally peeled back the layers to find the version of me who once had to make sense of it all to keep the visiting vicar happy. 'To me,' I said, 'it sounded like they were about kindness.'

Jim raised one eyebrow.

'Go on,' he said.

'And looking after people. Meeting their basic needs. And this makes God happy, I think.'

I waited for Jim's verdict.

'Well done, Charlie, you got a tiny part of it, al-though you put a sneaky socialist slant on it, being from Europe. I guess you people can't see that the greatest kindness is to allow the individual the opportunity to thrive free of government interfer-ence. Still, maybe you won't be a snake all your life.'

He smiled, as if he'd won a battle. I had to take control away from him, right away.

'So how do you square all that, then,' I said 'with what I understand to be your attitude to your own sister's condition of HEROS. That her hands are somehow sin themselves, and you and your family cannot touch them or things she has touched.'

He rolled his eyes. 'Here we go,' he said.

'Is that kind?' I continued. 'Would you say that is being kind?'

'I can't help that being the situation,' he said, deliberately. 'Yes, I believe that Alex's hands, if you want to call them that, are sin. It's not unkind to keep your distance from someone or something if they're dirty, or diseased, in the same way you don't hang out with a leper—'

'But hang on,' I said, a memory of school assembly stirring. 'Wasn't Jesus always hanging out with lepers?'

'Jesus had immunity!' he snapped. Out of the corner of my eye I saw Alex laughing behind her sinful hands, so I guessed he'd said something stupid.

'But what leads you to believe that Alex's hands are made out of sin?' I said. 'There's nothing about HEROS in the Bible is there? No one had it then.'

He just looked at me. He had no comeback. Improbably, I had him on the ropes.

'That is such a stupid point that just shows your ignorance,' he said, finally. 'There's no point to this conversation. I'm going to end this here.'

He stood up quickly, with the intention of making a dramatic exit on his stilt-like legs. I decided to press on, pushing myself up out of the ridiculous armchair and following him, knowing that Laura would go with me, no matter where it led.

'I just don't understand how you can say that HEROS is something to do with sin when it's not mentioned in the Bible.'

Jim turned around impatiently. 'What comes out of a person is what defiles them. Mark 7, verse 20. You see now?'

'No,' I said, knowing I was doing the trademark bemused look I reserved for such occasions.

'These… things that come out of people. Alex's hands. The feet. The wings. The tails. They are coming out of them and defiling them. What comes from within and defiles? Sin comes from within and defiles! Adultery, bestiality, homosexuality, like Alex here. Do I have to draw you a diagram, Charlie?'

'It might help.'

'It *comes* out of the body, Jim?' said a voice from the armchair. 'Quite sexual imagery you're using.'

'You watch your filthy mouth in your parents' house, Alex.' Jim's face turned a shade redder, his eyes filled with a murderous intensity.

'Does it rise up? Does it spurt out?' Alex continued to mock. I felt a change in the atmosphere. A worm turning. But also a sense that Alex didn't quite know what she was doing. She was having fun, making fun of her brother's sexual hang-ups, but the button she was pressing was not the one she intended.

'OK, we're really done here,' said Jim, manically heading once more for the sliding doors, as if to remove himself from the situation for his own safety. 'You have five minutes to get your stuff together and get out. You too, Alex.'

'This isn't your house, Jim,' she said.

'No, but I have a duty to protect Mom and Dad from harmful elements like you and your friends here.'

'Hey, Jim. Catch!'

Alex threw one glove, then the other, at Jim's face and walked towards him.

'Get back, Alex,' he said.

'Don't do anything silly, Alex,' I said, not totally meaning it.

'Oh, I won't,' she said, raising her hands. 'My brother just looks a little stressed out, so I'm going to give him a good... rub!'

And with that, despite being a good foot shorter than him, with a series of netball player leaps, she ran her hands swiftly over his face and neck, while he swallowed the urge to punch her on camera.

'Get off me!' he barked, in a strangulated voice that pitched strangely upwards.

'Ah, relax. It's just sin on my hands, bro. Don't you ever have any on yours?'

'There is no sin on my hands!' shouted Jim. With that, he gave in to his rage and grabbed Alex by the wrists.

'Ow!' she cried, partly in pain, but with an edge of delight that she'd pushed him so far.

'Let go, Jim,' I said, pointlessly, as I pondered whether Laura and I together could pin him down somehow.

The sliding doors opened. Alex's mother and father stood in the gap, confusion on their faces as they watched their adult son and daughter grapple with each other.

'What is going on here?' said her mother.

'You know we don't like you fighting,' said Michael, a dim remembrance of when he was the man of the house crossing his mind.

Jim did as he was told and let go of Alex. She went in for one last teasing rub over the top of his head, before dropping her own hands to her side. But as he did so, although I could have been wrong, and the camera did not pick it up, it did look to me that one of her hands lost its solidity, became intangible, and might have slipped inside her brother's skull, just for a second. Although if it did, he did not seem to notice.

They both stood there a moment, as if not quite sure how to explain themselves. But then something happened to Jim. He sunk to his knees. And let out the strangest sound. It was not a cry. It came from too deep down for that. A bellow, almost, like a lost animal calling to its mate. It did not stop.

Gingerly, his parents walked towards him, as if approaching a malfunctioning home convenience. His mother placed her hands on his head. His father patted his back. The noise did not stop. Alex looked confused, as if she'd scored a victory she wasn't planning on and wasn't sure she wanted.

'What have you done, Alexandra?' said her mother, looking up with disappointed eyes.

The noise broke down into sobbing.

'I think we should probably just go,' I said. Laura,

who had already stopped filming, gave me the thumbs up.

As we put our shoes on in the hall, I could hear that, through his sobbing, Jim seemed to be saying something, over and over again.

'I'm all sin, Mom,' it sounded like. 'I'm all sin...'

HEROS ON THE MARCH

We were silent for a moment in the car back to Alex's hostel. Normally after such an intense encounter, Laura and I would be laughing and yelling in our own way, just to release the pressure. But with Alex in the car, this wasn't possible. Sitting next to her in the back as Laura drove, I'd asked her if she was alright. She'd nodded, but it was clear that she wasn't in the mood for talking.

I was in two minds about what we had just recorded. Jim's collapse was so extreme we almost certainly couldn't use it in the documentary, despite having his signature on a release form for everything we filmed. Also, I hadn't actually got the footage I wanted of Alex interacting with her parents, which was what we were after in the first place. Still, the interview with Jim was very much usable. One thing was troubling me though. What had we witnessed, really? Had Alex somehow done that to him, accidentally or purposefully? And if so, was it with her mocking words and actions, or something else? Now wasn't the right moment to probe, but I knew it was something I would have to come back to later.

After a few minutes, the silence got too intense for Laura, and she put on the local rock station. The sound of hair metal pulled Alex out of her slump, and she headbanged nonchalantly.

'Well,' she said, finally, 'that was one big mind-fuck.'

'Mixed bag,' I said.

'Yes,' she said, mimicking my accent. 'Mixed bag.'

I geared up to probe further, but Alex raised her hand to stop me.

'No, let me ask you a question, Charlie. When you badgered me into going along with this for your great little programme, how much thought did you put into the risk you were pushing me into taking? I mean, you sold it to be as some sort of super-duper healing exercise for me and my parents, but did you consider at all that things might not go well? That they might actually get worse?'

I tried to speak, but she stopped me again. Her arms were waving with agitation as she spoke, her body pulled as far forward as the seatbelt would allow.

'Wait, I'm not done yet. I want to know how it feels to be you, Charlie. How it feels to just go round, collecting little human dramas starring people like me, and just sucking them up as fuel for your show and for your career. No, don't speak.

I'm just getting to the good part. You know what you would be if you were a rosie? You'd be an absorber. You'd be like the ones who can stick their fingers in power sockets and eat electricity. But instead of electricity it would be people's pain. You'd just stick your fingers everywhere, eating up all the pain, and making more pain so you could eat it, and the more pain you ate, the more powerful you got. They'd call you The Super-Absorber. So, there you go, Charlie, that's my question.'

She collapsed back onto the headrest, her seatbelt relaxing. Only the sound of hair metal and the low rumble of the car engine filled the space.

'That was more a statement than a question,' was all I could think to say. I immediately regretted it. Alex didn't hear me anyway, I don't think. She was crying.

Laura turned the radio off.

***

By the time we got back to the hostel, we had reached an uneasy truce. I had acknowledged that I was some sort of parasite, and Alex had accepted things probably would have gone better and more as I intended if her brother hadn't unexpectedly been there.

In advance of the demo, Alex, some flatmates and friends were to gather and eat Chinese takeout in the hostel lounge beforehand. Most of those there were Alex's age, and some sported a similar look to her, wearing combats and dog tags round their neck. In their minds, it seemed, they really were going to war. Some, however, were older, and some were notably straight-laced, one wearing a V-neck jumper not dissimilar to Alex's dad's. Some of their enhancements were visible. The spine of one, a young man named Marian, one of a number of foreign national rosies who had gravitated towards downtown Merriweather in search of a community, had elongated into a long, flexible tail that ended in a ball of spikes like a medieval morning star. Another, Kenzie, had shoulder blades that came with a small pair of fleshy, featherless wings she mostly kept tucked away in a comfy cardigan. The wings were non-functional, although there were rosies with larger wings that did have the power to lift them off the ground a few metres. Raymond, on the other hand, the man with the V-neck, was a glider. The flaps of webbing linking his arms to his body did allow him to catch air currents and glide short distances, although he said he found maintaining control very hard, so only did it in open spaces in the countryside. Nevertheless, he had broken his leg twice attempting it, and so his interest in gliding had waned over time. Elsewhere in the room was an older woman, Abbie, whose feet were so long she had developed a new way of standing on her toes, adopting the position of an animal on its hind legs. Her husband, Brett, was also there. He was not a rosie, although he was the first black face I'd seen in the predominantly white town. Besides these were various others who between them would spark, glow, become magnetic, stand several centimetres off the ground on a bed of hot air, ripple and vibrate. Still more didn't manifest their power in any visible way, but nevertheless had diagnoses of HEROS. And then there was Alex's girlfriend, Gina.

Gina was taking an MA in Political Theory, and threw around phrases like 'dominant privilege' and 'agentive action' with abandon. Now she sat cross-legged on a cushion at the centre of the room holding court in a pair of big red-rimmed glasses and a large jumper she pulled over her knees, her hair corkscrewing in all directions as if tapping into the minds of all around her. Although I found it difficult to believe many of them could follow what she was saying that well, there was something about the stridency with which it was said that made it difficult not to listen with at least half an ear.

'Sure,' Gina was saying to Abbie, one of the few present with the education to keep up with her, 'what you're doing could be categorised as rightful resistance in the classical sense, in that you are demanding that existing equality laws are being respected. But inevitably, when challenging physiotypical ordering from a marginalised, if not liminal position...'

And all the while, Alex lay sprawled out in front of her like a cat she occasionally stroked, sometimes gingerly making the beginning of a point for

Gina to talk over and ignore. Seemingly outspoken in every other circumstance, Alex was hesitant in front of her girlfriend, deferring to her with her nervous laugh and a mumbled 'sorry', as Gina stole what little thunder she could muster. Every so often, Gina would hold out a plastic cup for Alex to fill with juice as her mouth got dry from continuous talking. Otherwise, Alex would roll her small spliffs which Gina would smoke herself. These seemed quite inconsiderate, if not downright cruel, tasks to give someone whose hands could turn immaterial without warning, and I could see in her face that she was concentrating very hard on not dropping anything. It was certainly an act of dedication, if nothing else, but it was striking to see someone as outspoken as Alex reduced to the level of a near silent gopher out of sheer infatuation.

I took an immediate dislike to Gina. The way she had co-opted the oneders as a vehicle for her own theorising seemed narcissistic, while her lack of appreciation of Alex, reducing her to subservience and silencing her own not-inconsiderable voice in favour of her own actually made me slightly angry. But then, I noticed that much of what Alex had said to me about her struggles was in effect a more straightforward version of Gina's spiel. Maybe Alex needed Gina, I considered, to give her energies some focus. And as for Gina exploiting the movement, I thought back to what Alex had said about me in the car. Was I any less guilty? Wasn't I absorbing them in order to make myself stronger? Was I any better than Gina? And considering my reach in comparison to hers, following that logic, I was quite possibly much worse.

Speaking to various oneders gathered there, it was clear that what they wanted was quite basic. Opportunities to work, and financial support when they couldn't. An environment that was adapted to their needs. A level of basic respect and dignity. There was nothing much different from the demands made by various minority groups over the years. Except of course, members of this minority group might sport tails, wings, electricity-draining fingers and have the ability to pass through solid objects. As one earnest-looking young man whose eyes only saw in ultraviolet put it to me, 'When people see a oneder in the street, they can actually be disappointed. They're like, why aren't you using your power for the good of mankind, or whatever, because that's what the movies have primed people to think we should all be doing. But who knows, maybe we can get to that, if we choose it, if you provide us with a stable and suitable living environment first. Be a hero for us. Then, maybe one day, we'll be a hero for you.'

I talked with them about some of the other aspects of society's relationship with HEROS, as Laura worked to keep the longer communal spliff that was being passed around out of frame. When you're out and about, are people scared of you, I asked Marian, with the tail. 'Yeah, but the weird thing is it's hardly ever kids. It's always older people. I guess kids are just curious most of the time. They come up and ask about the tail, and I tell them that one day it was just there and they're fine with that. They know I'm just some guy who happens to have a tail. But maybe some older people can't think like that. They're more, well, you don't just wake up with a tail do you? He must have taken some drugs to make that happen, or, I don't know what they think! But that's the way it was. I woke up one morning, the bottom of my spine was on my bed, and I had this tail.'

And do they ever get called names? Between them, they gave me quite a list. Thing. That. Monster. Weirdo. Freak-face. Supercrip. Afterbirth. Abortion. Orangutan. Dagger dick. Chicken wings. Squinty.

Does it ever turn violent, I asked. Are they ever assaulted on the street? 'You're kidding, right?' came the reply, from numerous directions. 'Rosies are constantly being attacked. There were three rosies *murdered* last year here in Merriweather. *Three*. That's why we almost always walk in groups.'

And were they any social advantages to having an enhancement? Raymond, the glider, smiled. 'I definitely get more attention from girls since I got these,' he said, indicating his webs. 'I mean, let's face it, they're a conversation starter. They want to know about them, touch them. I get that a lot.' He winked and grinned at me for several seconds to make sure I got where he was coming from.

'Yeah, but you're a guy,' said Kenzie with the wings. 'It's different for you. I mean, I get guys coming up to me to talk about my wings all the time, and they're all like, oh, you're an angel, and it's just annoying. That's why I have them hidden away a lot of the time. I couldn't sit and read a book in peace before I got these, and now it's... And sometimes it's clear that they're into them, I mean really into them, like a fetish thing. And that is so demeaning. I do not want to go along with that. At. All.'

They ask me questions too. They want to know why I'm filming in the USA. Are there no hotspots in the UK? There are, I tell them, but I have to admit that filming in the US helps international sales of the documentaries significantly. The rosies in Merriweather are far more bankable than the ones in my local hotspot of St. Albans.

'Hey, we're box office!' said Raymond.

Gina was still talking to, or more accurately at, Abbie, who long ago had ceased even trying to defend her corner in the discussion.

'So, what you're really suggesting here is some sort of body-centred anarcho-syndicalism, which could not hope to succeed within the current ideological matrix, because—'

Alex gently touched Gina on the arm.

'We should get ready,' she said. 'It's nearly time.'

Gina sighed, obviously annoyed at being interrupted. 'Fine,' she said, smoking the end of her final joint before heading out. 'Let's get ready to kick some physiotypical ass.'

You're a physiotypical ass, I thought to myself as she sat there on her cushion as others sprung into action around her. I helped distribute some placards, including the one I helped make myself. I was quite pleased with how it turned out, even if I did go outside the line a few times.

***

Outside, they began to march. I joined them, and asked Alex if we could walk with her and film her reactions to what was going on. The plan was to make their way down the high street and to the town hall where they would disrupt the council meeting. The police hadn't been informed, and the roads were not sealed off, and I worried that we were in danger of being hit, accidentally or possibly, considering the level of hostility towards the rosies, deliberately by a car. Alex seemed unconcerned.

'Let's just say we have protection against that,' she said.

As more protestors joined us, making the numbers up to about a hundred, and we turned onto the high street, the chanting began.

'2, 4, 6, 8. Who do you accommodate?

'3, 5, 7, 9. Rosies say what's yours is mine!'

Another went, 'What do we want? The impossible! When do we want it? Now!'

I didn't really get the chants. They sounded like the sort of critical theory I read and didn't understand at uni the one year I was there. Looking about, interspersed, of course, with the odd insult thrower, I could mainly see confused faces on the sidewalk. It didn't seem that anyone knew what this march was about. I asked Alex who thought the chants up.

'Oh, Gina did,' she said. 'They're good, huh?'

I looked around before I spoke. Gina was ahead at the front of the march.

'Ah, to my ears they seem a bit obtuse, that they're perhaps not likely to make sense to the everyday person in the street. I mean, look at that guy,' I said, pointing at a baffled-looking man watching us. 'He has no idea what you're on about.'

'Oh,' said Alex. 'Well I think they're OK. And could you think up any better ones?'

'Maybe not,' I said. 'But you could.'

Alex shook her head in disbelief. 'Yeah, right.'

'You could, Alex. You've got a way with words. You could come up with something better, right now.'

Alex went quiet. I imagined a fight in her head between Alex the outspoken agitator and Alex the loyal, subservient partner of Gina. Then, cutting through Gina's bad chants, I heard her voice.

'Jobs are rosie! Shops are rosie! Everything's rosie in the rosie zone!

'Cars are rosie! Bars are rosie! Everything's rosie in the rosie zone!'

She gave me a glance. I reassuringly stuck my thumbs up. It needed a bit of work, but it was definitely an earworm.

The other marchers' voices dropped out to listen. The second time around, I gave a bit of support and joined in, nudging Laura to help out too, which she did, with an eyeroll. The third time round, other voices were chanting too. Fourth time, nearly everybody. Gina looked livid.

After a while, Alex simplified it to 'We want a Rosie Zone!' which summed up the point of the march so succinctly, it was probably what they should have started with. And it worked. The people gawping on the sidewalk no longer looked confused. Rather, they were talking amongst themselves, trying to get to grips with the idea being proposed. The insults still kept coming, but they were less. And while a trail of cars was building up behind us, angrily beeping their horns, this small crowd of rosies suddenly felt quite a powerful place to be.

As she was now chant-leader, I nudged Alex up to the front of the march and followed. Gina was nowhere to be seen.

'Guess she had somewhere else to be,' said Alex, sadly. I had an awful feeling that due to my manipulations to make the march, and therefore the programme, better, I had inadvertently brought an end to Alex and Gina's relationship. Then I realised that I wasn't that sorry, whatever principles of observational journalism I had no doubt violated.

The police were waiting for us outside the town hall. Not a full riot squad, but a handful of officers in their everyday uniforms. Merriweather was, after all, not that large a town, and probably ill-prepared for unannounced civil disobedience. Nevertheless, this being the US, I could see that they were armed, and my mind raced to where this situation may potentially go. Tear gas? Rubber bullets? I had no idea what they had in store or what was even possible, and by the look on some of the police officer's faces, I wasn't sure they did either. Some looked hostile, others seemed to be taking care to exude calm. Most, however, looked slightly afraid. But afraid of what? Just an unruly crowd in general, or a crowd of rosies? I looked back at the marchers. Despite all their sparking, small flames, tails and horns, they did not seem to me something to be fearful of when part of an armed unit. The rosies' 'powers' were mediocre, almost all useless in a combat situation. None of them seemed to have the capacity or the will to inflict serious damage on anybody. But still, there was fear in the police officers' eyes.

A commanding officer stepped forward, looking for a ringleader to address. At first his eyes set on me, but I shook my head and, as Gina had disappeared into the night, I felt the only thing to do was point at Alex.

'OK, guys,' said the officer, trying to find the right tone between reasonableness and utter inflexibility, 'you've had your little demonstration, and that's great, because we all love freedom of speech, don't we? But what I absolutely *cannot* allow you to do is go into the town hall. Any attempt to do so will be met with force.'

Alex's gaze turned steely and committed. 'We have a right to be in there. Those meetings are open to the public. There is a visitor's gallery for that purpose.' As she spoke, it felt as if all the anger and frustration she felt towards the world and, I liked to think, towards her absent girlfriend, was funnelled into those few sentences. It was the fury of the righteous.

The officer struggled to remain impassive, but his eyes darted like a man scanning his brain for answers. If he ever had been trained to handle a situation such as this, he had evidently forgotten what it was he had been told to do. Until very recently, Merriweather was not a 'protest' type of town.

'You *do* have the right to enter, but what you do not have the right to do is disrupt, and it looks to me that is what you have planned. So, I'm telling you, do not attempt to go inside, and it is now time for you to disperse.'

'Disperse? We're not going to disperse!' cried Alex, and began another of her chants.

'Rosie rights! Rosie rights! We want our own zone now!'

The rest picked it up quickly, with the volume escalating as it made its way back through the demonstration. The officer was handed a bullhorn, and used it to talk to Alex, even though she was just feet away.

'Tell your friends to disperse now, young lady, or there will be consequences. I repeat, there will be consequences!'

Alex's anger was struggling to be contained. I saw a vein in her forehead throb and her eyes go wide. She stepped forward towards the officer, and, as I'm sure I heard the soft click of the safety lever of a handgun, she raised her hand and spread out her fingers.

I grabbed it. 'Alex, no!' I shouted.

She darted a look at me, which in its split second of existence, told me that she knew what she could do with her power, and if what happened to Jim was an accident, then what happened to the next person, be it the police officer or me for daring to stop her, wouldn't be. But still, she put her hand down, and allowed me to pull her back, and no weapon was fired.

'Maybe it would be best if you called it a day,' I muttered to Alex. 'I'm not sure these guys are that in control of themselves. It could get messy.'

Alex smiled out of the corner of her mouth.

'Bring it on,' was all she said.

From beyond Alex's chant, another made itself heard. Violent, angry voices. 'Freaks out! Freaks out!' they said.

From either side, there were clusters of civilians, punching the air as they screamed at us. Young jocks mostly, enjoying the chance to blow off steam. But also, a mother with a child in her arms, a man in a well-tailored suit, and two mechanics from a nearby garage still in their overalls. A handful of senior citizens, one in an electric vehicle. They looked angriest of all.

Seemingly unafraid of the police, perhaps presuming they were on the same side, one of the jocks shook up a can and threw it at the demonstrating rosies, foaming beer spiralling out as it cartwheeled. I expected people to step back and clear a space where it would land. In fact, no one did. Even though at least some of them must have been aware of it, considering the pantomime the jock made of throwing it, none of the rosies seemed that concerned. I flinched as I awaited it to land painfully on someone's head.

But it did not land. Instead, the can somehow changed trajectory, going back the way it had came, landing with one final spurt of fizz at the feet of the teenager who had thrown it. Perplexed, he shook up another can, and his friends did the same. The assault of four flying cans had the same result. All got only halfway to their targets before returning, one catching the shoulder of one, making him yelp in surprise.

'What's going on?' I asked Alex.

She smiled.

'Yeah, it's the craziest thing. Turns out if you get enough rosies together, all the energies intermingling or something creates a kind of force field.'

'I didn't know that.'

'No one outside the rosie community did until now. So now you've got a scoop.'

'Seriously, can nothing get past it? Not even bullets?'

She raised her eyebrows.

'Maybe we'll find out tonight,' she said.

'Please don't say things like that.'

'Don't worry, Charlie,' she said, laughing. 'I'll save you.'

'That wasn't what I meant,' I said.

The returning beer cans had just made the jocks angrier, and they and similarly enraged observers were looking for more things to throw. When two of them attempted to uproot a recently planted tree, they found themselves hit by a blast of feedback from the police bullhorn, mixed with a demand they cease immediately. Chastened, and perhaps realising that the police were not going to allow them to drunkenly attack a minority any longer, they stepped back.

Alex looked around at the growing discomfort from both the police and passers-by, as the potential power of the rosies as a group dawned on them.

'You know what?' she said. 'I think we've made our point. They'll have heard us in there.' She gestured at the town hall. 'So what say we go crack open a few beers, huh?'

The rosies cheered at the word beer, and turned around, laughing and chatting amongst themselves as they began to walk back to their various homes and hang-outs. Alex blew the policemen a kiss as she went.

I stood back a moment and marvelled at the new Alex. When I had met her, I had presumed her to be good-natured and over-earnest, despite her veneer of cynicism. By inadvertently removing the shackles of Gina, I had somehow pushed her somewhere else. Before, she had seemed helpless, dropping things in supermarkets and getting upset about it. Now, she radiated power. I wondered about what I had done.

***

Back at the hostel, I'm afraid to say I got very drunk. The oneders were very happy with the impression they had made and, I think, being free of Gina's influence. They could be themselves now, and that was something more exciting, and full of potential, than they had realised. A party was in order.

Although she would deny it, and she definitely handled it better than I did, Laura was hammered as well, and we got very little usable footage from that night. What we found going over it back at the hotel was much whooping and singing, and a drinking game where everyone had to use their enhancement to make a pyramid of beer cans. Any attempt by me to ask a question came out nonsensical and slurred, and Laura's camerawork was too wobbly even for our naturalistic style, so we agreed that it would be best if we just wiped the footage. Which we did, except for one shot, that I wanted to keep. It was Alex, stepping outside on the porch for a moment, smoking a cigarette, looking at the moon, almost as if she were staring it down.

***

The following morning, I woke up on the floor, a coat placed over me like a blanket. Next to me were Laura's boots, standing upright as if she had just stepped out of them, although she herself was nowhere to be seen. Various sleeping oneders were draped across couches and armchairs. One with enormous ears was spread-eagled across the floor, snoring heavily.

My stomach churned, and I fought the need to be sick, while a feeling of absolute stupidity overwhelmed me. This was the sort of childishness I descended into without Sam around. Not only had I got drunk, I'd also failed to say no to the seriously strong skunk that was passed around. And if someone had laid out a line of coke, I knew there was no way I would have said no to that. Why didn't Laura stop me? Maybe because she was not my babysitter and she knew it would be funnier not to. The feeling of idiocy would follow me around for the rest of the day, I knew, along with my hangover.

A visit to the bathroom, and I found that I was

not the only one suffering that morning. Being a good houseguest, I cleaned up after myself and, by the look of it, several other people too. I looked at the time. It was early, but we should have been going. We weren't even meant to be there at all. I set about looking for Laura, but first I had some unfinished business.

I knocked on Alex's door and gently called her name.

'Go away,' came a voice, after a minute of knocking.

'It's Charlie,' I said.

'I know,' she groaned. 'Go away.'

'Can I come in?'

'Why are you not getting the whole go away thing?'

'Just for a second.'

Alex opened the door. She was wearing a dressing gown and a pair of ridiculous slippers in the shape of cartoon hippos.

'What?' she says. 'They're super-comfy.'

She let me sit down on the bed.

'I just wanted to say goodbye,' I said. 'Because I'll be going in a second. Thanks for having us.'

She smiled, genuinely.

'Hey, no problem,' she said. 'It's been... Fun isn't the word I'm looking for.'

'I've had fun,' I said.

'Yeah, but for me, it's been more... educational. I've learned stuff.'

'I think you have,' I said. Our eyes met. I was

suddenly very aware that the person I was talking to was only superficially the same as the person I'd met the same before. She hadn't just grown. She'd somehow evolved.

'But I'll come back, if that's OK, to follow up, see how things are going, before we wrap up shooting.'

'Yeah, whatever. It's a blast having you around, Charlie. Everybody here loves you. Except the guy with the ears. He thinks you're an asshole. Nah, just kidding.'

'Listen, before I go,' I said. 'There's something I want to ask.'

'There's always something you want to ask, Charlie.'

'Seriously, though. Yesterday, at your parents' house. Just before Jim had his, ah, episode, shall we call it... I thought I saw your hand go maybe, I dunno, a bit intangible and slip inside him, just for a moment. Would I be right in saying that?

She blinked quickly. She was thinking, I could tell.

'Maybe I did,' she said. 'I don't remember.'

'And if you did, would that have been an accident... or on purpose?'

'Like I said, I don't remember. And if I had, it would have been an accident. Obviously.' Her gaze was hard now. She was learning fast.

'Because last night at the demonstration, I thought you were going to do the same thing to that police officer. Make your hand intangible and put it inside him. And maybe have something similar that happened to your brother happen to him.'

'I don't know what you're talking about. Why would I do that? When my hand is like that, it does *nothing*. That's the problem. God, for a journalist you really don't pay attention.'

For a moment, I felt like I was back with the Alex I'd first met. Or someone doing a good impression of her.

'Sorry, Alex,' I played along, sensing I wasn't going to get anything more out of her, and all I could do now was maintain our relationship until the next visit.

'You know,' she said, 'what happened to my brother was really nothing to do with me. It's… the thing is, he's not really my proper brother. I mean, he is, but my dad's not his dad. Mom was pregnant with him when they got married. My dad saved her reputation, you get me? And Jim had no idea for years, until, I dunno, it came out somehow when he was in his teens, and then… He went weird, really religious. Got it into his head that because he was a bastard, then he was just pure sin or something. And that's when he started going from church to church, trying to find one that would agree with him, I guess. Until finally he washed up in the church he's at now, that has these cray ideas about HEROS, and I think it makes him really happy, because now he's not the one made of sin. His little renegade sister is.'

'So,' I said, trying to make sense of the implications of it all, 'when he says your hands are sinful, do you think he's projecting? That it's really him that's the sin that came out of, well, your mother, because of the sex out of wedlock thing?'

'Yeah, I think that's it. But I didn't think about what I was doing, and I reminded him, and it all came out and then he was just screaming... so, yeah.'

It was all so neat. It was almost convincing, as much as that kind of psychobabble ever was. But I wasn't buying it. Still, I gave Alex a hug, and left her to her hangover.

I found Laura barefoot in the kitchen, making coffee for assorted worse-for-wear oneders.

'You look like shit,' she said.

'I feel like shit.'

Laura looked like she'd spent the night in reading a book.

'We should go,' I said.

'Yeah, I'm just waiting for you to be sick,' she said.

'I've been sick already.'

'You'll need to be sick again.'

'You know me too well, Laura,' I said.

She poured me some coffee, and I felt my stomach churn. I ran to the bathroom.

HEROS AT WORK AND PLAY

Lizabeth shows me some of her toys. She talks about them in the style of a YouTube unboxing video. 'This is Mary Muffin. And this is Rainbow Bite. They're both quite old toys, from Season Ten, which means they came out one year ago. But this is Eggo Waffle, and she's Season Twelve, so she's new, and comes with accessories. You can position her in several different ways. Let me show you…'

In many ways, Lizabeth is an absolutely average eight-year-old. She likes to play with her sister, Summer, around the house and in the park. She goes pony trekking regularly, and enjoys theme park rides. But Lizabeth does not go to school. Instead, she has a private home tutor, which her parents are just about wealthy enough to be able to afford. And when she does go out, she wears a helmet which obscures most of her face. Not because her head needs protecting, but simply because other people's reactions tend to be so extreme, that the family has decided they are not worth the effort of dealing with.

Lizabeth is one of the youngest people ever to be diagnosed with HEROS. Two years ago, when she was seven, Lizabeth's bottom lateral incisor teeth, those either side of her middle pair, both dropped out simultaneously. Although most children lose these teeth at this age or soon after, this was not quite as it should be. For instead of making way for her adult teeth, these missing baby teeth were almost immediately replaced by another set of teeth entirely, leaving the adult teeth still intact beneath the gum. These new teeth were long, large and alarming to look at, like those of a wild boar. They pushed up against Lizabeth's upper lip, distorting the shape of her mouth, and extended right up in a curve to just underneath her eye. She has to sleep with corks on them to prevent injury.

Lizabeth's speech was hard to follow, and her mouth could not contain her saliva. But none of that mattered when she was talking about her beloved toy collection. She seemed a happy child, and I enjoyed playing with her. She came up with all sorts of imaginative, funny scenarios for her toys, and I thought other children would enjoy her company too. I wondered how much contact she had with other children.

'Yeah, she attends various clubs, not just for HEROSic kids, but for children with various disabilities and additional needs,' said her mother, Jenny, a homemaker who appeared to enjoy nothing more than providing a good environment for her two

slice off some flesh.'

'I won't get too close, if you don't mind,' I said.

'No, I don't mind at all,' he laughed. 'I wouldn't recommend it.'

Wayne does not have a left arm below the elbow. Instead he has a long, bone blade that looks slightly like that of an old plane propeller. It is unbelievably sharp. Wayne has deep indentations in his right hand from before he realised just how sharp it was. Analysed under an electron microscope, the cutting edge of the blade was seen to be just one molecule wide.

Most of the time, Wayne keeps the blade in a sheath with an inner lining of lightweight metal. Even so, the sheath is heavy, and tends to pull him down to one side. He has back issues because of this.

'So, were you a butcher before this, or…?' I asked him.

'No. I was a chemist actually. But that wasn't really tenable after… well, after this thing turned up!'

He lifted the blade to make his point, and I flinched as it moved, even though I was feet away and in no danger.

'What makes HEROS-sliced meat better than meat that's been cut with a more usual blade?'

'I haven't a clue!' he laughed. 'You'd have to ask the customers that, but they swear they can taste the difference.'

'Could it taste… sharper?' I offered.

'Yeah. That's it! It tastes sharper! Good one!' He laughed again, and used his blade like a hacksaw to break the carcass's spine.

***

I don't think it would be right to say I got into TV by accident, but I didn't exactly apply for the job. A schoolfriend who I used to mess around with making stupid videos when I was fifteen had his heart set on being a comedian, and just in to my second year of uni, studying for a humanities degree so vague I can't even remember what it was, he got back in touch. Some production company was looking for fresh talent for a sketch show and he needed an audition tape. One of the things we used to do on our home videos were silly interviews where I'd play a clever broadcaster talking to some member of the public who was an idiot. It wasn't an original idea. Very Monty Python, very Pete and Dud. But I got to sneer, which I was good at, and that made it entertaining, to us anyway, so we dredged it up and did it again with a few more years of cynicism on top, and sent the tape in.

My friend got a letter. They thanked him for his interest, but he wasn't what they were looking for. But while they had his attention, would it be possible for him to provide them with my phone number?

OK, I got into TV by accident.

They didn't want me for the sketch show. Instead, they saw me with my very own programme, going round talking to strange and unusual people who thought and did odd things and sneering at them. I thought about it for a full six minutes. It would, after all, interfere with my plans of coasting non-committedly through life for as long as possible..

Ah, to hell with it, I thought. This was what I was born for. I said yes, dropped out of uni, and never spoke to that friend again.

***

'How does this affect the, ah, romantic side of your life?' I asked Wayne. He seemed a good enough sport for that sort of question. 'Does it affect things, say, in the bedroom?'

'Well, no one's got hurt so far!' he said. 'As long as I keep the sheath on, it's not a problem.'

'It's always safer if you use a sheath,' I said.

'Ha! Good one!' he said, slapping my back with his regular hand.

Then he withdrew the blade from its cover again. For a moment, I thought maybe I had upset him, and I was in real trouble. I glanced at Laura. She shrugged, as if to say if I did get cut there was nothing that she could do about it, and kept on filming.

'Hey, watch this!' he said, and sliced a slab of meat at speed. 'Your average butcher would have to use a meat slicer machine to get cuts like that...'

'But you can just do it with your blade.'

'That's right.'

There was a loud clang.

'Ha! Would you look at that,' he said, looking at his handiwork. The blade had gone right through the meat and made a large dent in the metal surface underneath.

He dipped his blade in a big tub of disinfectant. Then he looked at the dent again. I looked too, and saw it wasn't just a dent, but he had sliced clean through, leaving a gaping slit that looked like some awful metallic wound.

'Never done *that* before! Ha! Would you look at that?'

I very much wanted to get away from Wayne and his blade.

'I think we've got what we need, Wayne,' I said.'

'Are you sure you don't want to see how I make sausages?'

***

I was visiting the couple I had met the other night at Alex's, Abbie, the woman with the very long feet, and her husband, Brett, at their home. Shoes were a problem for Abbie, and she only owned a couple of pairs of specially made ones she wore sparingly, going barefoot much of the time. In her own home she liked to wear what were meant to be knee-length socks. Stripy and thick, they only reached her ankles.

'Do you get a lot of attention as a couple?' I asked,

as we stood in the kitchen, drinking lovely fresh coffee, Abbie towering a full foot and a half above the rest of us.

Brett smiled. 'Yeah, we were kinda getting that anyway,' he said.

'Because of the race thing.'

'Correct. You do not see a lot of black people in Merriweather. And you do not see a lot of mixed-race couples.'

'It's just us, actually,' laughed Abbie.

'So has HEROS affected your relationship in any way?'

'I wouldn't say so,' said Abbie. She turned to Brett. 'What about you, hun? Would you say it's made anything different?'

A broad grin broke out over Brett's mouth.

'Oh,' said Abbie. 'I don't think we should tell him about that…'

'Tell me about what?' I asked.

They both just stood there, grinning at me.

'Is this… something to do with the bedroom?'

'Shall we tell him?' Brett asked his wife.

'Let's show him,' she said.

**

Taking full responsibility for my own decisions, I nevertheless have to say, the reason I was rotten to women so long before I met Sam, cheating on my partners constantly and using as many for sex as would let me, was because of my mum. I found that out in the compulsory therapy sessions I did in rehab that turned me into such a truth addict.

For the earliest years of my life, I loved my mum more than anything, like you're meant to. She always seemed to be smiling, I think she hugged me often, and I remember my little mittened hand in hers. As I grew older, though, it seemed as if the smile was a mask. I began to notice it didn't feel altogether real, and her eyes often gazed into the distance, as if there was something coming over the horizon. Then, one day, when I was eleven, she held a family meeting for me, my little seven-year-old brother and my dad, where she grandly announced that she was leaving, to live somewhere else, with another man, and another ready-made family. I still don't know if my dad knew she was going to say this or not, as his face didn't move the whole time. And with that, my mother was soon gone, and I knew that every single smile, every single hug, every kindness, had been fabricated, and I had never meant anything to her at all.

I thought my dad would pick up the slack and we would become closer, but of course he sent me and my brother to boarding school so he never had to think about us except during the summer holiday and Christmas, something I guess factored into my brother's Christmas Day suicide attempt seven years later. As for my mum, I saw her intermittently out of a sense of propriety, I guess, and even though her new family ejected her after a couple of years for reasons she didn't feel worthy of discussion, she never said she was sorry, or gave any indication that she was. Just still the smile that was a mask, and the eyes looking at the horizon for something that was coming.

And from my first kiss on, I stretched myself in two different directions, somehow breaking other people but never myself. I longed for the closeness of someone who could be my partner, holding my no longer mittened hand in theirs, but I would never let anyone cast me aside like that again. So I sabotaged every relationship, and chucked every one night stand out of bed in the morning with just enough taxi fare for them never to come back.

Everything changed when I met Sam. At last, this was someone I sensed wouldn't and couldn't do what my mother did to me. And because of that, I couldn't do to her what I had to all the others. And that's when I finally started living.

My mother died of cancer last year. The shock wore off quickly, and after that I was simply glad.

***

Brett lay on the carpet of their lounge, while Abbie crouched over him, raising herself up and down on her toes, her long arches giving her an extra bounce. They were fully clothed, simulating the extra dimension HEROS had given their sex life, and laughing hysterically.

'That look like fun, Charlie?' said Abbie.

'You think you'd like that, Charlie, huh?' beamed

Brett.

I smiled, politely. I had seen a lot of strange sex stuff over the years, and most of it was too niche and weird to tempt me that much. Despite my promiscuity, when it came to the actual act I was very boring. Tiresomely heterosexual and un-fluid, anything more than the basics seemed like needless window dressing. But looking at them on their lounge carpet, I had to admit, it did look like fun. And then something unexpected happened. An unwelcome, and unprofessional surge. I never responded in that way when working, even when I was interviewing women who were practically naked or the talk was about sex. It was just the wrong mindset for that. But there it was, down there, making itself known.

'I expect it's very nice,' I said, noncommittedly, hoping the denim of my jeans was thick enough to hide what was happening. I realised it had now been some days since I had had sex, and I was now regretting not sorting myself out in the hotel room when I'd had the chance. But this was how dead I was after a day's work now. Too tired even for that.

**

That evening, Laura and I had decided enough time had passed for us to go back to Bo's and try and wheedle some more material out of him. Maybe I could get him to crack this time, or maybe I could squeeze something sad out of Paynter. I'd left

Laura to phone and set up a time for filming, hopefully as soon as possible.

I then phoned Sam, catching her just before she
went to bed. I masturbated while I talked to her
about Abbie and Brett and the other people we'd
seen, and as she talked to me about her working
day and a row her sisters had. I didn't mention
what I was doing, but I think she probably knew.
I'd done it before, and she'd caught me out. She
could hear it in my breathing, she'd said. I breathed
quieter this time.

***

I was woken up from my oversleeping by banging
on my hotel door. Bleary eyed, I opened it to Laura.

'What's up?' I yawned.

'I just phoned Bo's,' said Laura, full dressed and
ready for action, her serious, professional director's face on. 'Talked to Paynter. There's been a
development.'

'What do you mean?'

Laura swallowed.

'Bo's... he's gone to Stage II.'

'Oh god,' I said, feeling the blood drain from my
face. 'That's absolutely terrible news.'

'Yup. It's downhill all the way for them from
here. There's no coming back from this. Stage II,
Stage III, Stage IV, and then... That's how it's going
to be.'

'God, I can't believe it. This is so utterly dreadful…' I thought through the implications. All of them. 'Are they still going to let us film?'

STAGE II

HEROS IN METAMORPHOSIS

Paynter sat hunched on the step of the house. Any brightness that emanated from her had gone now. She rocked as she spoke, and wouldn't make eye contact.

'Can you tell us what happened?' I asked, sticking my finger in the fresh, open wound.

'It's difficult to…' Her voice trailed off into nothingness. I waited for her to collect her thoughts, hoping it wouldn't take too long or we'd have to make an awkward edit. 'It was when I came back from dropping Mason off at soccer practice. He was standing there, in the living room, and… I don't know. He just looked different. He kept on looking past me, at the door, like there was something he was hiding from, or didn't want me to know about. Then he grabbed me by the shoulders, like hard, looked at me, like, really intense, and he said…'

She drifted away again. I couldn't wait so long this time. I needed to know and the viewers needed to know.

'What did he say, Paynter?'

'He said, whatever anybody else says, I needed to know that he wasn't... that he wasn't...'

'Wasn't what?'

She took a deep breath, mucus dislodged from crying heaves crackling in her chest.

'That he wasn't... The Trout.'

'The Trout?' My tone was wrong. I sounded incredulous.

She nodded. 'The Trout. Yeah. And then I just knew. It had happened.'

'Stage II.'

'Stage II. Yeah.'

I didn't say anything. We needed a pause now, as I let Laura capture my concerned face in a lingering silence, soon broken by a low rumble and the tinkling of glass from the kitchen. Something fell, and broke.

***

Bo was in the living room, sitting on the sofa, bolt upright. He was wearing his usual comfy home clothes and crocs, but he did not look remotely relaxed. His eyes darted, as if on the lookout for unseen enemies who might leap out from behind the furniture at any moment.

'Hi, Bo, how's it going?' I said.

He said nothing. His eyes kept darting.

'Are you OK?' I said. 'You look tense. Would you like me to pour you a glass of your Scotch, perhaps, to relax you?'

His eyes caught on me, seemingly noticing me for the first time.

'I guess you heard, Chad,' he said, finally, his voice a monotone.

'Heard what?' I said.

'What people are saying about me.'

'No. What are people saying about you, Bo?'

'They are saying — and I can't believe they're saying this, it's so unbelievable — but they're saying that I'm The Trout.'

'The trout? What's the trout?'

'Not what. Who. He's a crimefighter who has been seen in these parts. Silvery suit. Looks like a rainbow when it catches the light. Helmet like a trout's head.'

'And people are saying you're The Trout?'

'Yeah. It's ridiculous. I'm not The Trout.'

'Who's saying this, Bo?'

He blew out his cheeks, 'Everybody. Just everybody. The neighbours. Guys at work. Paynter hasn't said it yet, but I can tell that she thinks it.'

'I don't think Paynter thinks you're The Trout, Bo.'

'Nah. She's got the look in her eyes. The look everyone else has when they... well they don't even have to say it out loud. You can tell that's what they think.'

'Has anybody said it out loud, Bo? Or do you just think they think it?'

'Well they may as well have said it out loud! No difference, as far as I can see, between looking at you like that, and saying it!'

He glared at me intently, emphasising his speech with a slap of his thigh.

I saw no point in pushing it any further. I'd learned from years of talking to people who believed odd things that you can't argue someone out of their delusion.

'I don't think you're The Trout, Bo,' was all I said.

'Thank you, Chad,' he said, grabbing my shoulder. 'That means a lot to me.'

I felt his tension release a bit, and I thought we were about to enter a moment of relative calm when a cry from upstairs tore through everything.

I darted towards the hallway, but Bo somehow managed to leap from the sofa and get through the door before me.

'Don't look in the closet, Paynter!' he shouted, desperately, bounded up the stairs, three steps at a time, before diving into the master bedroom.

When Laura and I got there, Bo was on his knees, clutching his head.

'It's not mine, Paynter,' he cried. 'You've got to believe me!'

Laura was standing by the closet, sobbing. At her feet was a silvery wetsuit that glinted with colours where it caught the light, and some sort of helmet, crudely fashioned out of a cardboard cereal box, with the dead eyes and features of a trout sketched on in felt-tip pen.

***

It took a long while to get Bo calm enough to sit back down on the sofa. Me and Laura told him repeatedly we did not think he was The Trout, and when Paynter had collected herself in the bathroom for ten minutes, she did too. This was the recommended technique for dealing with those at Stage II of HEROS. Bo had already spent some time being assessed by a specialist earlier that day. There would be a further visit tomorrow. Inevitably, as his delusion increased and he became more and more agitated, he would be heavily tranquilised much of the time.

We sat with Paynter back out on the step.

'Are you going to be OK on your own here, tonight?' I asked. The children, Mason and Skiff, were staying at a relative's for a few days.

She nodded.

'This is just the way it's going to be from now on,' she said. 'May as well get used to it.'

'You really don't have to be alone,' I said, only half-thinking about the footage we could get if we stayed.

'Oh, I've got neighbours I can call on. And we're going to get regular visits from HEROS Support. I'll be fine.'

She smiled, stealing herself up for the life she

would now be leading, of a carer for a man in the grip of the delusion that he was secretly a costumed crimefighter called The Trout.

**

We both hugged Paynter and left her there, sat out on her step.

I felt that we had turned a corner in our investigation. There would be no more feel-good stories like those of Brett and Abbie, or Wayne the butcher. We would be going on a different route from now on.

Laura felt it too. We always got to this point, somehow, whenever we filmed.

'Time to go to the Dark Places?' she said.

'Time to go to the Dark Places,' I replied, as Bo's rumble, now seemingly beyond his control, radiated out behind us, interrupting the smoothness of the drive with its loose stone vibration, and a sharp jabbing pain behind both our eyes.

HEROS DEFINED

I was in the surgery of Dr. Candice Wexler, a specialist in HEROS, relocated from Boston to Merriweather after it became classified as one of the largest of the 210 hotspots in the US, to operate a free clinic. A stern woman who looked like she was tired of my questions before I even began, I tried not to take up too much of her time.

'How would you define HEROS?' I started. A nice, easy opening question for someone like her.

She frowned.

'How would I define it?'

'Yes.'

'Don't you have a working definition already? This information is freely available online, you know.'

'Yes, but if we have an expert say it, then it adds an air of authority for the viewers. If I just say it, then they'll just think, well he's googled that.'

Dr. Wexler sighed.

'Fine,' she said. 'HEROS is a disease that affects cellular regeneration, causing new organs to grow while forcing existing ones out of the body. The new organs often have characteristics not previously found in those of human beings. In a significant number of cases, nearly 40% of males, although just under 20% of females, the disease then attacks the brain, causing a series of delusions that invariably impede on the mental health of the sufferer to a severe degree.'

As she spoke, she sarcastically bobbed her head from side to side, like a schoolgirl being made to recite memorised tables.

'Do we know what causes it?' I said.

'No.'

'Are there any theories as to what might be causing it?'

'None that are worthwhile. Background radiation, pollution, spores from an unknown fungi… No evidence for any of them, but they get some of my colleagues on TV, I guess.'

'You're on TV now.'

'Well, yes. This place is funded entirely by donations. So if any of your viewers have any spare change they want to throw my way, please visit my website, www.wexlerherosclinic.com. But I'd be very happy not to be on TV.'

'Yeah, I get that. So what makes HEROS so fascinating, do you think?'

She sighed a still bigger sigh than before. It was obviously the wrong question again, but I doubted there was going to be a right one.

'Whether I or anybody else is fascinated is really beside the point,' she said. 'It's a serious condition with no known cure, that causes an incredible amount of distress in the lives of the sufferer and those around them, and needs to be treated the best we can. And that's why I'm here, in this miserable, boring town, helping these people, instead of running my own private practice in a city I actually enjoy living in. In Boston, I was just down the road from a boulangerie that made the best French bread. Have you tasted the bread here? I mean, have you? No? Well, it's bad. Now, do you have any other questions?'

I wasn't sure what a 'basilisk stare' was, but I was pretty sure I was getting one right then.

'No, I think we're done.'

I was standing up before Laura had even stopped filming.

***

'I didn't do anything wrong, did I?' I asked Laura as she drove us away. 'I didn't ask anything I shouldn't have done.'

'I know that usually the answer to that question is yes,' she said. 'but this time you actually didn't do anything wrong.'

'So what was that all about then?'

'Some people are just dicks, I guess.'

'But she's providing free healthcare for those who can't afford it. So she's actually better than us.'

'Yeah, life's complicated that way.'

'Can we use any of what we filmed?'

'Nah. Just say it all yourself in the voiceover.'

***

The next stop was a day centre for people at Stage II of HEROS. Here, relatives could leave them for a time to act out their delusions of deception and discovery, while taking a much-needed break. The centre was based in a small disused college campus.

Kerry, a volunteer carer, showed us around.

'What's really important about this place,' she said, leading us down a long corridor, 'is that there are a lot of unused rooms.'

'Why is that important?' I asked.

'I'll show you,' she said, opening a door. 'We keep them all unlocked, because, well, you'll see.'

We stepped inside. It was an abandoned seminar room, empty save for some stacks of chairs and a whiteboard, fallen from the wall and now propped up against it.

'Now, just in here, we have several premium hiding places. If you care to look behind here...'

Kerry pointed at the stack of chairs. Lodged between them and the wall was what looked like parachute silk. She pulled it out. It was a costume, brightly coloured. It came with a cowl, on the forehead of which was some sort of 'third eye' logo.

'And there's another one, here, look.'

Tucked between two of the stacked chairs was a second costume. Jet black, seemingly made out of bin bags, except for a pair of green gardening gloves with the fingers cut off.

'And I would not be at all surprised if... ah, here we are.'

Kerry pulled the whiteboard forward. Behind was a third costume. This one looked profession- ally made. Some kind of leatherette fabric, in browns and oranges, a large sunblast on the chest.

'So what do you do with these?' I said.

'Oh, we just leave them,' she said. 'They'll sneak in and move them somewhere else later.'

Kerry scanned the room one last time, obviously aware of where all the potential hiding places were.

'OK, I think we're done in here,' she said. 'Do you want to see a therapy session?'

'If that's possible? It wouldn't be an invasion of privacy?'

'Absolutely not. It's actually helpful to have wit- nesses.'

She led us out the room. Outside in the corridor, three men were hovering, buzzing with agitation. They all immediately spoke at once in a cacophon- ous babble that would occasionally sync up on key phrases.

'Whatever you saw in there, whatever she told you, you need to know, I am not The Yellow Sun/ The Wall Crawler/ Mind Man, you just have to be- lieve me!' it sort of went.

'Just ignore them,' whispered Kerry. 'You can't do anything with them when they're like this.'

'They're all saying the same thing, pretty much,'

I said, as we walked away, their loud voices bouncing down the hall after us.'

'Yeah, but that's what Stage II does to you,' she said. 'They all end up more or less the same person.'

'It's all a lie!' the three men shouted in unison as we turned the corner.

***

'I believe you,' Kerry was saying to the young woman sat facing her. 'You are not what they say you are. There is no way you are the crimefighter known as Radio Girl. The costume that was found in the toilet cistern is not yours. You are a wonderful, beautiful, creative person with nothing to hide.'

She held her hands and looked directly her, her face not far from hers. The woman was nervous and twitching, but as Kerry spoke, her movements lessened, and her eyes got caught by Kerry's gaze for longer.

All around the room, volunteers were doing the same thing. Sat closely with Stage IIs, they tried to look into their darting eyes and say reassuring things. Although there was still the odd paranoid outburst, and none of them could be said to be calm, the service users could definitely be said to be in a better place than they were at the start of the session.

'How long does this help them for?' I asked Kerry,

quietly.

'Oh, anything from five minutes to five hours,' she said. 'We know it's always going to be very temporary, but it stops the mania from building to boiling point so frequently.'

'It's like a release valve,' I said.

'Yeah, or a massage.'

Kerry gave her attention once again to the young woman.

'You are so great,' she told her. 'You know that? So fun to be around. Really pretty. And honest. I'd believe anything you said about anything. Hey, can you give me a smile?'

The woman's eyes darted away. Then, cautiously, she turned her head to Kerry, and smiled.

It was a beautiful moment. It seemed as if she hadn't smiled in a long time. It lasted until a blast of radio static came out of her and she frantically pulled her hands away from Kerry, placing them over her now tightly shut mouth.

'It's OK,' said Kerry, cradling the young woman's head on her shoulder as she cried. 'It doesn't mean anything. There's no way I think that makes you Radio Girl. It's someone else. It's OK…'

***

'What I don't understand,' I said to Kerry, as we wrapped up our time with her, 'is that some of the costumes we saw hidden away today looked pro-fessional. I mean, they looked as if someone who knew what they were doing had designed them, and they had been made to order. Why is that?'

'They look professionally made because they are professionally made,' she said, giving me the continuity link I needed.

'By who?' I asked.

'There are companies who will make costumes for Stage IIs.'

'For money.'

'Of course.'

'And Stage IIs commission these costumes just so they can hide them?'

'That's right.'

'And what do you think about that?'

'I think it's exploitative and disgusting. But what can you do?'

She smiled helplessly. I shook her hand.

HEROS FOR SALE

Joanne Scheider is the brains behind HEROSsories, an outfitters that provides bespoke crimefighting costumes. Besides this, they also help their customer refine their overall crimefighting concept and look. Working from the customer's own ideas and sketches to produce a costume that wouldn't look out of place in a Hollywood movie. Based in a smallish space in the one building that comprises Merriweather's garment district, the company is mail order only, but lack of shop space does not affect public awareness. Their advertising is everywhere in Merriweather. On billboards, the sides of buses, and on every local TV channel. There is zero chance of any HEROSic people at Stages I-III missing it.

Joanne had agreed to show me the process, and so I found myself leaning over a drawing board in the company's design department, looking at a crude drawing in felt tip pen that looked as if may have been done by a child. It was of a mostly green stick man with a long tail, claws, and two rows of teeth coming out of his head.

'So what is this?' I asked.

'This is the initial idea for a costume that the customer has had for their costume. As you can see from the drawing, they are tail-endowed, and not surprisingly, they've gone for a lizard theme for their crimefighting identity.'

'Do they have a crimefighting name in mind?'

'At the moment, they want to be known as Lizard Man.'

'Is that a bit obvious?'

'It *is* a bit obvious, and we might gently suggest they go with something a bit more subtle, a bit more upmarket.'

'Such as?'

'Such as, maybe, simply The Iguana, or something a bit more mysterious, like Night Lizard. Whiptail…'

'I like Night Lizard. That's quite menacing.'

'Yeah, I like Night Lizard too. I will probably suggest that to him.'

'Because there are probably a lot of Lizard Men out there already.'

'Right.'

'How do you think up the names?'

'Wikipedia. There's a list of lizards.'

'Is that all there is to it?'

'Can you think of a better way?'

'No,' I said. 'I guess I'd go on Wikipedia too.'

We turned once again to the drawing.

'I mean, this is very basic, isn't it?' I said. 'It's a stick man with a tail, pretty much.'

'It is basic, yeah,' said Joanne. 'But there's still a

lot to go on. We know he wants to go green, have the costume cover the tail, and go with a cowl. So we have colour and shape right there.'

'And what do you do with that?'

'Well, we pass it over to one of our dedicated designers, such as Katie... Hi Katie!'

Katie waved to us from the other side of the room from behind her drawing board.

'And what Katie does is turn this initial idea into something like... this.'

Joanne slid another piece of paper onto the drawing board. It was a truly remarkable drawing, in the style of Golden Age comic book artists, of a costumed crimefighter. Recognisably the figure from the stick man sketch, here he was fully fleshed out, fists flying and tail snapping, face partially obscured by a lizard-head mask.

'Wow, that is amazing,' I said.

'So then we just translate this concept art into some flat sketches like this...'

She slid over another piece of paper, this one a plan of the costume complete with measurements.

'...and we take it through here.'

Joanne led me through a pair of double doors into the workshop. Here, several young people, fashion students by the look of them, were cutting and sewing together material in various striking colours. I picked up an offcut of material for the benefit of Laura's camera and examined it.

'What is this?' I said, pulling it. 'It's very stretchy, and springy, but it's very thick. I don't think I've seen anything quite like this before.'

'That is what we make all our costumes out of, and it's a synthetic fibre that was actually created by NASA and it's called Hidron.'

'Hide… as in hide of an animal?'

'That's correct. It's intended to be, like, a thick second skin for astronauts.'

'Why would they need that?'

'I don't know. You'd have to ask NASA! Anyway, I bought a job lot of it a while back because I could see the potential. It has all the qualities you're going to need from a crimefighting costume.'

'Which are?'

'Well, firstly, it's stretchy, which is important, because we're dealing with a lot of different body types. *And* it's flattering. No one looks too bad wearing this.'

'Because just because you feel you need to dress up like this, you're not necessarily going to have the physique for it, is that what you're saying? You might not be that muscly and you might have a few wobbly bits but in this, it doesn't really matter that much.'

'Correct. There's just something about this material that really works with what we're doing. You kinda look like you've got muscles wearing it, even if you haven't, and it lifts the bits of you that need lifting.'

'So what other qualities does it possess that are useful to you?'

'It's thick. And tough. I mean, we can't cut it with

scissors. We have to use an electric knife. Our sewing machines are the most heavy-duty there are.'

'And why does it matter that the material is thick?'

'Because if they, you know, end up out on the streets, dressed like this, it protects them.'

'Just how tough is it?'

Joanne shrugged.

'It'll absorb a punch pretty well.'

'Stop a knife?'

'Maybe. Depends on the knife and the person using it.'

'Stop a bullet?'

'I'd better say no because there's no way we could guarantee that.'

'But it might do?'

'I'd better say no.'

I noticed some green fabric being stitched together on a particularly large and noisy sewing machine.

'Is that the Lizard Man costume there?'

'Yes, it is. We're making it now, it'll be finished in, I'd say, half an hour. The tail takes a long time to do. You need a fair amount of stitches on that to give it rigidity. Otherwise it kinda droops down like a saggy bag and that's a bit sad.'

'While we wait then, can you tell me about the other aspect of the service. Because you don't just make costumes, do you? You also provide an overall look.'

'Yeah, we help them accessorize.'

'Accessorize?'

'I'll show you.'

We followed Joanne into a store room. Cardboard boxes lined the shelves. Joanne showed us what was in some of them.

'Here are some little masks, for the crimefighter who doesn't want a cowl. Metal armbands and gauntlets are very popular for those who are going for a more old-timey, say, Medieval look... And these rings with big, colourful stones in them are popular with both women and men who want a magic vibe.'

'Is this the extent of the look management? Little bits of costume jewellery?'

'Not quite,' said Joanne, rummaging in another of the boxes. 'Because every crimefighter has their devices, right? So these are little light things they can distract their enemies with. We call them dazzlers.'

I picked one up. It was a small red disc that that lit up with a flashing LED light when you pressed a button.

'It's a bit like a bicycle light,' I said.

'It's a dazzler,' said Joanne, moving to another box. 'And these are throwing stars. They come in lots of different colours. Like, here's a green one. Lizard Man could have some of these, and they could be things he shoots from his lizard claws or something like that.'

I picked one up. It was tinted green but it was also metal and also very sharp.

'But these are weapons! Are you allowed to sell these?'

'They're ornamental.'

'Oh, come on. You must be aware of the dangers of giving someone with Stage II HEROS something like this.'

'You can order these off the internet, or buy them from a specialist martial arts store no problem. If they don't get them from us, they'll get them from somebody else.'

'But you know what they're eventually going to do with them, Joanne.'

'They're ornamental.'

I have found that sometimes, once you have asked one awkward question, there's really nothing for it but to follow it up with another.

'How much do you charge for all this?'

'Prices vary but we start at $5,000.'

'$5,000? That is a lot of money.'

'Well it is to some people. But you get a lot for it.'

'You get a costume.'

'You get a whole new identity. A new you. I'd say that's worth $5,000.'

'But aren't you exploiting people with what is essentially a mental illness? I mean, the main symptom of Stage II HEROS is a delusion, and you're facilitating that.'

'We are providing them with a service that makes their experience of their condition as comfortable and rewarding as possible.'

'Their experience of their condition? They're not

going to a theme park!'

'No, they're not. But anyway, Stage IIs are only a part of our customer base.'

'But they are part of your customer base.'

'Yes, but only a part of it. We also sell costumes to Stage Is who use it as part of their livelihoods or are just a bit flamboyant, those with Sympathetic HEROS, and just general HEROS cosplayers.'

'But you do sell to Stage IIs though.'

'Yes, we do. And I don't see a problem with that.'

'Because?'

'Because of the reasons I've already given you.'

***

I thought we were going to get thrown out after that exchange, but we still hadn't got footage of the finished costume. No doubt seeing the opportunity for a free advertisement, Joanne agreed to let us stay for the next twenty minutes until it was finished.

Laura popped outside for a cigarette, and I followed her. I hadn't smoked for years. Sam had weaned me off. Now the smell of it made me slightly sick, but I never lectured Laura about lighting up in front of me. I knew it wouldn't go well if I did.

'It's just awful,' I said. 'Making all that money out of people's illness.'

'Yeah, and you're doing this for free,' said Laura, in between drags.

'That's different.'

'How?' she said, provocatively blowing a smoke ring near my face.

'I'm not charging any HEROSic people for interviews!'

'No, but you've been doing this long enough to know what you do, what I do, is all about. We take all the weirdness people can't help and we've turned it into our careers.'

'Maybe in the old days,' I said. 'But we're raising awareness now.'

'Providing a service.'

'Providing a service.'

Laura exhaled a large cloud of smoke. Her way of telling me she'd won the argument and no further discussion was necessary.

***

'Wow,' I said, at the finished Lizard Man costume. It certainly was impressive. Emerald green, almost glowing in the light, with authentic-looking fibreglass claws and teeth, and a tail that was certainly rigid.

Joanne smiled at her workshop's creation.

'Worth $5,000, don't you think?'

I didn't know what to say.

'Wow,' I said again, eventually.

***

As Joanne had said, HEROSsories did indeed sell many costumes to Stage Is. Although most used them for financial benefit, there were some who simply liked wearing them. Landon, or Starflower as he liked to be known, was one of those.

We met him outside a bar in the downtown area. With skin so pale I suspected he was an albino, in his star-shaped sunglasses, bright yellow leotard, glittery platform boots and headdress that looked like the rays of the sun, behind which sat a large dyed-blonde afro, he slightly resembled a seventies glam rock musician.

'You're certainly dressing to impress,' I said.

'I prefer dressing to *ex*press,' he said, with a smile that was somehow both friendly and defiant at the same time.

'Do you dress like this every day?'

'Oh, yeah. Well, if I don't dress like this, I don't go out.'

'How many costumes do you have?'

'Six. One for every day of the week.'

'But there are seven days in a week.'

'I'm saving up for the seventh day.'

'Are they all the same or is each one different?'

'Oh, well, you might say they look the same, but a true costume connoisseur could tell they are not. The little differences in cut are very important to me. I talk through every detail with the designers.'

'Do you have a job to pay for all this?'

'Oh, I can't tell you how I make my money.'

'Someone give it to you?'

'If I did have benefactors, I couldn't possibly talk to you about them. That would be indiscreet.'

'Why do you do it, Landon?' I asked. I noticed that passers-by jeered and abused him with striking regularity. 'It seems a hard path to choose, in some ways.'

'Because — excuse me. Do you go down on your momma with those lips, buster? Uh, what was the question?'

'Why do you do it, dress the way you do?'

'Because this is who I am. And it doesn't matter what these bozos spew out of their potty mouths. I'm not ashamed, and I'm telling the whole world. This. Is. Me.'

'Would I be right in saying you're gay?'

'Maybe you're right and maybe you're wrong. This is nothing to do with my sexuality. I'd dress this way whatever I was into. It's about being me. And who I am, what I am, is spectacular. You want to see something? Watch this.'

From behind his headdress came a brilliant glow. His whole scalp was illuminated, his afro becoming a somewhat frizzy lightbulb.

'That is amazing,' I said.

'And I can get it a whole lot brighter, if the moment inspires me.'

A small crowd had gathered round. A group of college age girls giggled and reached out gingerly to touch Landon's hair. He bent down obligingly. A spark flew out to a finger, and the girl jumped back with a delighted shriek. They touched all the more, hoping for another spark.

'Yeah, I'm gay,' he said to me eventually, 'but do you *know* how much pussy I could get, just standing here?'

***

Unlike Landon, Don Wilson does not wear a costume simply to express himself. For Don, it is strictly business.

'So who are you in this?' I asked him. 'What role do you play?'

'I am The Pummellor.'

'Is that a word?'

'Yeah, it's a word. Means I pummel things.'

Don was wearing a vest and tights made out of Joanne's Hidron, along with some of the Roman-looking gauntlets and armbands she had shown me, and a full-face mask that made him look more like a wrestler than a crimefighter. This was intentional, as Don The Pummellor is one of the performers in the HEROS Gladiator League, where Stage Is take to the ring and act out choreographed fights using their own particular replacement organs.

Like Alex, Wayne the butcher, and many others, Don's organ replacement affected his hands. His are now uncommonly large, definitely the biggest hands I have ever seen. Despite his best efforts, the weight of them pulls down his arms, as if he is constantly struggling with a pair of heavy suitcases. As part of his costume, Joanne had provided him with an enormous pair of gloves.

'Are those easy to get on?' I asked.

'Yes. Why wouldn't they be?'

'Because they're so large.'

'So are my hands.'

'Are your hands dextrous?'

'Dextrous enough to get a pair of gloves on.'

A buzzer in the dressing room signalled it was showtime. We followed him out and down the corridor to the stage entrance and the sound of the crowd chanting his opponent's name.

'Nervous?'

'Why would I be nervous?'

'You might lose.'

'I won't lose.'

'Does the script say you win?'

He gave me the dirtiest look. A sustained cheer echoed down the corridor for his opponent, who must have stepped out into the arena already.

'Script?' he snarled. 'There ain't no script.'

And out he walked to a wall of boos. The Pummellor was the bad guy in this scenario. We watched as he worked the crowd, shaking his enormous fists and pretending to argue with his enemy's fans in the front row.

In the centre of the arena was not a ring as you would expect in a boxing or wrestling match. Rather it was a dirt-covered oval, in a manner akin to old Roman amphitheatres. Scattered about on the floor were various fibreglass weapons for the fighters to pick up and use if their own innate power let them down. I spotted a sword, shield, mace and spear. They would be deadly if they were real.

The Pummellor's opponent, Third-Eye Slim, was waiting for him in the ring. A skinny man, his striped costume accentuating his slender frame, who had an actual third eye in the centre of his forehead, hidden behind a visor. As he limbered up, the crowd cheered him almost as loudly as they booed Don.

A dwarf in a loincloth struck a large gong, signalling the beginning of the fight. There was no referee. HEROS Gladiator League was renowned for not having any rules to speak of.

They circled each other for a while, Don occasionally going in as if for a punch, but then backing off as Third-Eye Slim pointed to his visor. Then, suddenly, Don went for it, running straight at Slim and hitting him relentless with both fists, with only a slight nod of the head beforehand to indicate he was going to do it.

Slim fell to the floor. Despite making apparent efforts to push The Pummellor off with his feet, Don kept on going. Then, reaching out one hand, Slim miraculously found a mace lying in the dirt. Nearly getting a hold on it, then not, then finally getting it, he swung it with all the might in his scrawny body and hit The Pummellor square in the head with it. Don staggered back. Third-Eye

Slim hit him again, and again. Don fell to the ground, and begged for mercy as Slim took several steps back, and lifted up his visor, revealing his third eye. A beam of intense red light shot out, illuminating Don's chest as he screamed as if in agony.

Slim lowered the visor. Don thanked him with praying hands, only for Slim to lift the visor again and shoot him in the chest again. Lowering the visor, they went through the charade for a third time, Don thanking him, only to be rewarded by another blast of red, glowing energy. At this point, The Pummellor ran from the ring, pursued by Third-Eye Slim, firing at his bottom. The crowd rocked with laughter. Don lifted his legs high like a cartoon character whose pants were on fire, a movement he dropped immediately as soon as he passed us at the stage door and entered the corridor back to the dressing room. Third-Eye's beam was harmless, a light show and nothing more.

Third-Eye Slim followed. He and Don slapped each other's backs and laughed for a second.

'That was a good one,' said Don.

'Yeah,' said Slim. 'They thought it was funny. Really good reaction to the story. Anyway, better wrap this up.'

Slim turned, and stepped once again back into the arena to lap up the crowd's applause.

'So Slim was saying they liked the story? Does that mean there's a script?'

'Script?' snarled The Pummellor. 'There ain't no script.'

***

Phoebe is a sex worker. An independent escort, she operates out of a hotel near the centre of Merriweather. Although she occasionally tours to New York City, Boston and Washington DC, Phoebe finds that for the most part this is unnecessary. People will travel to her, not only from all over the US, but from all over the world.

'Yeah, I've had them all come here,' she told me, in the lounge of the hotel, during a short break between clients. 'Saudis, Russians. Brits like you.'

'And why is that?' I asked. 'I mean, you're a very attractive woman, but what quality in particular is it that, ah, you possess that makes men fly—'

'And women.'

'Women come as well?'

'You bet.'

'...So what makes men and women fly halfway around the world to... spend time with you?'

'This,' she said, and stuck out her tongue. It immediately grew long and fat, impossible now to fit back in her mouth with ease. It somewhat resembled an octopus tentacle, lined with suckers that rose up out of the pink flesh and back in again. It corkscrewed into a spiral and tightened, and loosened again, the suckers moving in and out all the while. I had a no-doubt erroneous sense that the tongue had a mind of its own, as Phoebe had a faraway look in her eyes while this happened. Then, just as swiftly as it had expanded, it shrank back into the size and shape of a normal tongue, and slipped back into Phoebe's mouth.

'There are just three rosies with sucker tongues in the world,' she said. 'And I'm the only one who gives head.'

'And is it, ah, more pleasurable than normal oral sex?'

'Well, Charlie, what do you think? Does it look like fun to you?'

'It… it could well be.'

Phoebe leaned forward. 'Scientists came to check it out. They proved, scientifically, that my head is the best head *possible*, for a man or a woman.'

'How did they prove that?'

'They paid me to give them head, of course!'

'Is that scientific?'

'Apparently they paid a lot of other women to give them head, as a comparison.'

'That does sound scientific. So do you make a lot of money doing this?'

'Look at me,' she said, gesturing at her clothes. She was wearing a velour tracksuit and trainers. It was just about glamourous in a ghetto chic kind of way, but certainly not the usual outfit of a high-end escort. 'I make so much money, I don't even need to dress nice. I just lounge around in my sweats, give 'em head, and shove them out the door. I could wear a garbage bag, they wouldn't care. I don't even need to sweet-talk. They just want the tongue, that's all they want. That's all they *need.*'

I looked at Phoebe, trying to see her as some sort of tragic figure. But I knew she made much more than I did, or ever would, and it was her tongue that was really doing all the work. Perhaps I was falling for the 'happy hooker' fallacy, but she seemed, well, fine.

'So what about you, Charlie?' she said, perhaps realising I had run out of questions. 'Can I book you in for the scientifically *proven* best head in the goddamn world?'

'Oh, ah, I don't think I'd be able to claim that on expenses,' I said. 'And I've got a partner... girl-friend.' As I said it, I knew I should have mentioned Sam before the expenses. We'd obviously use it — it was TV gold — but it would make me look bad. I would get tweets.

'Well, if you change your mind...'

Phoebe's phone vibrated.

'My four o'clock's here,' she said. 'I gotta go.'

She shook my hand, and I watched her walk away in her velour tracksuit, knowing that Laura had her camera trained on me, catching me looking uncomfortable. I could hear her laughing.

***

'Can I see it?'

'Sure, man, sure.'

It had been some years since I had asked a man to show me his penis on camera. The last time it was because it was freakishly large. Theo's had other unusual qualities.

'Now watch this.'

Theo held it, flaccid in his hand, in the office of a downtown sex club, his boxers round his knees. He started pumping it, making it erect.

'Can we show an erect penis?' I murmured to Laura.

'If it has educational value,' she said.

'Oh, this is gonna be educational, alright,' said Theo, professional that he was, his member fully erect in a matter of seconds.

There was nothing to look at to begin with, and I wondered for a moment if we had been conned into filming someone's penis for no reason besides their self-gratification. Then, something happened. Ripples ran up and down it, intricate patterns of bumps and ridges rising and falling. It was strangely beautiful, and for a moment I forgot I was staring at another man's penis.

'Right now, it's just in screen-saver mode,' said Theo.

'What do you mean?' I asked.

'When that's in a woman,' he explained, proudly, 'it can detect exactly what she needs to stimulate her at that precise moment, in the right place, not just to the millimetre, but to the micrometre.'

'So it's like those condoms you get with knobbly bits on then, essentially.'

Theo looked at me, hurt.

'If that condom with knobbly bits on, as you call

it, could think, and achieve maximum satisfaction every time with every woman, leaving them fucked like they've never been before and never will be again, then yes.'

'I didn't mean to offend you.'

'You didn't offend me.'

'You acted a little offended.'

'Well, maybe you did offend me, a little bit. I don't like to be thought of like I'm an object. I'm a man. With an incredible dick. And my dick's not an object either. It's part of me.'

'I understand that. Can we talk about the moment you realised your, ah, organ, had been replaced? Presumably there must have been a moment when you noticed that your original penis had become detached from your body.'

'Right,' said Theo. 'I was at work. I was in security, at a shopping mall. And I just felt something slip right down the leg of my pants. And there it was on the shopping mall floor, my penis. Blood everywhere. Somebody was screaming. I was screaming, I think. And then I checked myself, and I was like, I'm alright! I still got a dick! And because I said that, I got fired.'

'Harsh.'

'It was harsh. But then I discovered what my new dick could do, and a lady or two found out what it could do...'

'You got positive feedback.'

'I got positive feedback. More than that, I got *recommended*. Before, I never got laid, man. Like once a year, or something. After, they were queuing round the block. Round. The. Block.'

'And now it's your job.'

'Now it's my job. Which reminds me. It's time to put my costume on.'

Unlike Phoebe, Theo could not get away with doing his job in sweatpants. Instead, he donned a costume he kept in a locker, provided, of course, by Joanne and the staff of HEROSserries. His was a turquoise affair, with LED lights embedded that sent a pattern not unlike the ones that occurred on his penis up and down his body. There was a hole in the groin area through which his penis and testicles flopped out.

'What name do you go by here?' I asked.

'The Rippler.'

'The Rippler. Excellent. Shall we go upstairs?'

'Yeah,' said Theo. 'Let's go upstairs.' He sounded less happy about it than I thought he might.

***

'Rosie Wallbangers' was a fetish club for heterosexual couples who sought to include Stage I males in their sex lives. Theo earned a good wage from the club's owners for providing this service, although the state's anti-prostitution laws meant that his declared role was simply one of 'host'. Theo was the highest paid of several hosts on duty that night, able to command more money as he was the only one whose abilities were centred in his penis.

'What is it that these couples want you to do?' I asked him, on the way up.

'Fuck the wife, all of them. Some of them want me to fuck the guy as well, but I ain't doing that. Should do, though. That's where the real money's at.'

'What does the man do, while you're having sex with his partner?'

'Sometimes he's getting blown by her, or we take it in turns fucking her. Sometimes he's playing with himself. Mostly, though, he just watches.'

'He enjoys the humiliation?'

'Yeah, the humiliation of seeing his wife having the best sex of her life with someone who's genetically superior to him, which he can never hope to match.'

'Do you consider yourself genetically superior?'

'For the purposes of the fantasy we provide here, you bet.'

'And when you're not at work?'

'I'll be honest, sometimes I wish I didn't have it.'

'You don't want to have the penis you have?'

'Sometimes. I mean, it's a crazy thing to be defined by, you know? Your dick. When I look back on my life when I'm older, is it really going to be enough to say I had a whole load of sex?'

'Many men would say yes.'

'Many men have never found themselves pounding the pussy of some grandmother at four in the morning when they just want to go home to sleep. I mean, you wouldn't believe who we get here. The mayor and his wife were here. Someone I went to school with's mom was in here. I was like, Hi, Mrs. Silverman!'

'And you had sex with her?'

'Yeah, it was my job to.'

'Was that hard?'

'Nah, there's stuff I take for the hard ones.'

'Viagra?'

'Yeah, and stuff.'

We passed through swinging doors and into the club. Already couples waited for The Rippler, lounging about on rubber mats covered in what looked like parachute silk. It reminded me a bit of a soft play area, but for very grown-up games. In an alcove, one of Theo's co-workers, a bat-winged rosie dressed up like the Devil, was having sex with a woman while her partner watched, transfixed.

'Better get to work,' muttered Theo, like a man about to step onto a building site, as he lowered himself onto the mats, the couples madly scrambling to get to him first.

He looked over his shoulder at me and shrugged, as a woman old enough to be his mother pumped his penis, waiting for it to ripple for her like she knew it would.

***

I talked to Sam on the phone that night. I masturbated as she told me about what was happening at her work, with our friends, British politics, celebrity nonsense. But after a while, I found I was not really listening to what she was saying. There were pauses in the conversation where I was clearly meant to be talking, but was not.

'Is something wrong?' she asked eventually. 'It doesn't feel like you're really there.'

'No, I'm here. I'm here. Keep talking. I like to hear your voice.'

And she did. But all the while she was talking, I was thinking about Phoebe and her tongue. What did it feel like, I wondered, to be sucked off by *that* thing? It had looked gross, but so had vaginas until I finally had sex with one. And the scientists had been right, hadn't they? It really was the best in the world. And just before I silently came, I thought about Abbie, her elongated feet giving her a little extra bounce as she rode her husband.

It was undeniable. I wanted to know what sex with a rosie would be like. It was an itch I could never scratch without destroying everything, but there it was.

'I'm guessing you came, then?' said Sam.

'What? No. How did you know?'

'I always know when you're jerking off when you talk to me on the phone. I can hear it in your breathing.'

'Damn, I thought I was getting away with it.'

'You can't hide things from me, mister. I know you inside out.'

She was right. She did really know me. There was no hiding anything from Sam. But I would hide this, I thought. I would hide it well.

HEROS BY ASSOCIATION

'I was sitting at my desk at work,' Hope was telling me, 'and I just knew, in that moment, that my old hand had gone, and a new one had taken its place. A hand that was a whip.'

'But your hand hadn't gone,' I said. 'The hand that you have now is the same as you had then. It isn't a whip.'

'According to your version of reality.'

'But it's the version of reality that's shared by me with almost everyone.'

'But it's my body,' said Hope. 'And it's my version of reality that counts when it comes to it.'

She smiled, in a manner that said, I'll answer your questions, but don't push your luck.

Hope has Sympathetic HEROS, a psychological condition where the sufferer believes that they have experienced an organ replacement, when none has taken place. While some theorise that Sympathetic HEROS is in some way related to

Phantom Limb Syndrome, like HEROS itself there is no real understanding of it at all. All that is known is that soon after the first cases of HEROS itself appeared, so did those of Sympathetic HEROS.

'Can you show me your whip?' I asked. We were sat in the living room of the house she shared with her husband, Lorne, and three children.

'Sure.'

Hope pulled out a long case, not unlike a flight case for a guitar, from behind the sofa, and opened it up. Inside was a shining metallic whip, made from a series of small interlocking joints, topped with a cover that could slip neatly over the hand, creating the illusion that it was an extension of the arm itself.

'Wow. And where did you get that?'

'HEROSsories. But it's really just the physical, visible version of the whip I know is there anyway.'

'Did you get anything else from HEROSsories?'

'Yeah, I got a costume.'

'And why did you get that?'

'To make the whip look good! Want to see it?'

'Please.'

'I'll be right back.'

Hope slipped out the door.

Her husband, Lorne, was hovering in the hall.

'Do you like the costume, Lorne?' I asked.

'Oh, yeah,' he said, grinning.

'Why is that?'

'You'll see.'

Several minutes later, Hope slunk down the stairs in a skin-tight Hidron catsuit, zipped down to reveal a lot of cleavage, high-heeled boots, and a metallic belt that mirrored the look of the whip.

'Get me my whip, Lorne,' she said, coldly.

'Yes, mistress,' he said. I had no idea in that moment if this was a game or not, and if so, if it was for our benefit or theirs.

Lorne presented her with the whip. She slipped her hand inside the cover, and let it drag along the last steps of the staircase, making a chinking sound as it went. She stepped into the living room regally.

'What do we call you when you're dressed like this?' I said.

'Hope,' she said. 'What else would you be calling me?'

'Ah, just because I felt there was some roleplay going on there.'

'Oh, that's just with Lorne. We've always had that aspect to our relationship.'

'I helped design the costume,' said Lorne. 'I just go all subservient when I see it. Can't help myself.' He giggled excitedly.

'Well, does it have a practical use?' I asked. 'Can you do Indiana Jones stuff with it?'

'Well, let's see,' she said. 'Hold still.' She pulled the whip back, as if to crack it.

'I didn't mean on me!' I cried theatrically for the camera, but also totally meaning it. 'It looks like it would really hurt.'

'It's not real metal,' she said. 'It's a polyurethane. It'll only hurt if you move.'

'I'm really not sure about this…'

Laura gave me a thumbs-up from behind the camera.

Hope cracked the whip, and it wrapped itself round my legs. She pulled on it and it tightened. I knew if she pulled on it any more I would fall head-first onto the floor. Instead, she let it go slack, and I could step out of it.

'That is impressive,' I said.

'Aren't I?' she said, before breaking into some sort of spontaneous gymnastics routine involving her whip, right there on the living room carpet.

'She's very flexible,' I said to Lorne, as she cart-wheeled perilously near the glass coffee table.

He waggled his eyebrows and smiled.

***

Sympathetic HEROS is a controversial issue within the rosie community. While some see those with the condition as fellow travellers, others view them as an unwanted distraction, muddying understanding of the problems faced by those with HEROS itself.

To explore these tensions, I decided to make another visit to see Alex and her friends. If anybody had strong feelings on the matter either way, it would surely be them.

'Hey, you know what we should do?' said Laura

on the drive over from behind the wheel. 'We should go in, talk to them, and have Hope sat outside in the car, secretly watching it on a live feed, then get her to walk in, catsuit, whip, tits out, and see what they say about her to her face.'

I knew Laura was joking, sort of, but not so long ago that's exactly what we would have done, in the Sneer Years.

'We can't do that,' I said. 'We don't manipulate. We document.'

'We would be documenting. We'd be documenting a situation we created. Just like we do all the time. Like you'd be turning up in these people's homes if you didn't have me following you round with a camera?'

'Oh my god. You're serious, aren't you? This is everything we've been trying to get away from for the past few years. Absolutely not. No.'

'It would be great TV, Chas.'

'The live feed is Reality TV bullshit. No way are we doing that.'

'What if we left out the live feed, and just documented her talking to them, with or without whips and tits? I mean, it's a debate, right? Why not get them talking?'

I put my head in my hands.

'Why do you do this to me, Laura?'

'Do what?'

'Have these ideas that are so good we have to do them?'

Laura laughed and turned the car around. I

phoned Hope to tell her to pack her whip.

***

Alex opened the door to the hostel.

'Hi, Charlie,' she said, smiling with a little less warmth than I was expecting considering all that we'd been through last time. 'Back again to mess with our heads.'

'Hi, Alex. How's it going? Can we go to your room so you can update us on your situation?'

'Actually, my room's out of bounds right now. I'm kinda working on something in there.'

'Ooh, a secret. How exciting.'

'Not really a secret. More none of your damn business.'

'OK, where shall we go then?'

'The lounge. Everybody's there.'

'Can't we talk to you alone first?'

'Why? We're a community. Why not talk to all of us?'

'Because you're our favourite, Alex.'

She rolled her eyes.

'Yeah, your favourite cow you can milk for material. Come this way.'

Alex led me through to the lounge. There, slumped in various sofas and the floor, were some of those I had spoken to the night of the march, including Abbie, this time without Brett, Marian with the tail, Raymond the glider, and the winged rosie, Kenzie.

Alex took Gina's old place in the centre of the room on the big cushion. I stood next to her, thinking she would offer me some space on it. She didn't.

'So, guys,' I said, addressing the room like a nervous supply teacher, 'I'd like to ask you how you feel about people who suffer from Sympathetic HEROS. Do you see them as fellow travellers, if you will, or—'

'Absolutely not,' Alex interrupted. 'Whatever they are, it's nothing to do with the actual experience of having HEROS. I mean, it's just playacting to them. None of them, not a single one of them, ever has to find out what it's like to live in a world for which their body, which might well be doing something crazy every other second, is not compatible. Anytime anything gets too hard, they can just take off their prosthesis or whatever they've got and carry on like the able-bodied person they are.'

Alex finished. No one said anything. Did she speak for all of them, or were they afraid to challenge her, I wondered.

'I actually disagree,' said Abbie, hesitantly. 'Just because they haven't experienced organ replacement in reality, doesn't mean that their perception of that having happened isn't as painful as our own. The way I see it, they are part of this situation, and they should be part of our cause.'

'No way,' said Alex.

'Do you feel sorry for them at all?' I asked.

'Yes, absolutely,' said Abbie. 'At least we can see our new body parts and come to terms with them. They can't even do that.'

'What about you, Alex?'

Alex shook her head. 'They're tourists in our misery. They should go get their own illness if they want attention so bad.'

I looked around the room. Still no one said anything.

'What if I were to say to you, that outside, waiting in the car, is someone with Sympathetic HEROS. And how would you feel about her coming in here now and meeting with you? Would any of you have a problem with that?'

Alex put her face in her hands.

'Oh, Charlie, did you go to night school to learn how to be an asshole, because you're *so* good at it!'

'As you keep saying. But would it be OK for her to come in and talk with you guys for a little bit?'

The room seemed to be waiting for Alex to answer for them, but she just stared at me open-mouthed in mock astonishment.

'Sure,' said Abbie, finally. 'I absolutely don't have a problem with that.'

A ripple of agreement went around the room.

'Fine,' said Alex. 'Bring them in. Do your exploitative little bit for your dumb TV show.'

'I really just want you to have a conversation,' I said. Alex blanked me and looked at her phone. Laura went outside to fetch Hope.

'You are *such* an asshole,' Alex muttered into her

phone screen as we waited.

Several minutes later, Hope walked in, her breasts falling out of the catsuit that was zipped down to the navel, pausing to pose provocatively in the doorframe with her whip. I guessed Laura had given her a little pep talk on how to behave, although she seemed happy enough to go along with whatever had been suggested.

'Guys, this is Hope.'

There was a mumble of nervous hellos as Hope offered her left hand for shaking.

'Oh, come on,' said Alex. 'You can't expect me to take this seriously. This is just pure exhibitionism. Don't waste my time with this, please.'

'Alex,' I said, 'why don't you address Hope directly. Tell her exactly what your problem is with what she's doing.'

'OK,' said Alex, taking a deep breath. 'What is going on here is HEROS blackface. You're presenting a crude caricature of us for your own narcissistic amusement. Do you see any of us wearing a stupid costume?'

Hope smiled. 'No,' she said, 'but I see a bunch of people who are comfortable with who they are, like me. Well, maybe not you. You seem a bit angry. Maybe you're not happy with yourself.'

Alex raised herself off the cushion and stretched herself up. Any attempt there may have been to intimidate was somewhat offset by Hope towering over her in her boots.

'I'm angry,' said Alex, fixing Hope with an uncomfortably intense glare, 'because the world doesn't take the needs of people like *us* seriously. And you're not helping, with your cheap porn outfit and your fake strap-on whip hand.'

Hope returned the glare. As a staring contest, it was an even match. I kept an eye on Alex's hand, just in case.

'To be fair to Hope,' I said softly, 'there are some HEROSic people at Stage I who do wear costumes. There is this man who calls himself Starflower. Maybe you know him…?'

'Yeah, we know Starflower,' said Alex. 'If that's what he wants to do, he's more than welcome, because, get this, he actually has HEROS.'

'Sympathetic HEROS is HEROS, hon!' cried Hope.

'No. It. Is. NOT.'

'I think it is, in a way,' said Abbie.

'Then you are mistaken, Abbie,' said Alex. 'You're scientifically, factually wrong.'

'That's a matter of opinion.'

'No! Facts are not a matter of opinion. That's why they're facts!'

'Maybe we could get a show of hands,' I said, hoping to break the tension that had gotten higher than I was comfortable with, although I could see Laura was loving it. 'Who here thinks Sympathetic HEROS is, pretty much, the same as HEROS?'

Hope and Abbie shot up their hands. A few other hands wavered, uncertainly.

'And who doesn't?'

Alex put both her hands up. A few more wavering

hands.

'And who's undecided?'

A sea of hands.

'Well, that's pretty conclusive. You don't know if Sympathetic HEROS is HEROS or not. So, where do we go from here?'

'You get out of my... *our* home, Charlie,' said Alex. 'And take this freakshow with you.'

***

'Freakshow? I can't believe she said that, the Symphobic bitch.' Hope was fuming in the back of the car as we drove her back home. 'Yeah, I'm an exhibitionist. Always have been. But I'm not Sympathetic to show off. I've just incorporated it into the showing off I was doing anyway. You think this is my first catsuit?'

'I'm sorry if that upset you,' I said. 'I wasn't expecting it to get quite so rough.'

'Don't be. Now you got it on tape, the whole world can see. This is the sort of bullshit we have to put up with, from physiotypicals and rosies.'

'Shot by both sides.'

'Exactly.'

She carried on, pulling apart Alex's position, but I was finding it difficult to concentrate. Things were changing for Alex and her friends. She herself seemed harsher, more dogmatic, less vulnerable. And now Gina was gone, she was fully in charge, despite Abbie's small challenges. I wanted to know how things would pan out for those guys, where she was going to take them. Alex was up to something she wasn't going to tell me about, and I sensed things were going to get interesting. A thought in my head began to grow into an idea.

***

Hope disappeared through the door of her house with a wink and a cheeky slap of her buttock with her coiled whip.

'Hotel?' said Laura.

I shook my head.

'I want to check up on Bo and Paynter,' I said.

'Why? We got all we need from them, haven't we? Save for wrap-up.'

'I don't want to film. I just want to see how they're doing.'

Laura sighed.

'You are not the Chas I used to know. You've gone so soft.'

'Soft in the heart?'

'Soft in the heart. Soft in the head. I don't know about anywhere else. I'd have to ask Sam.'

'But could we drive over please? I'll be ten minutes. You don't have to come in.'

'Hey, wherever you go, I go. I'm pretty much your bodyguard.'

'I don't pay you to be my bodyguard.'

'I don't get paid for any of this, Chas. I just do it for the thrills.'

'Yeah, right.'

***

'Whatever they say, Paynter, you've got to believe me. On my mother's grave, I am not The Trout. The costume under the sink is not mine!'

'You're not The Trout. Not your costume. Gotcha.'

Paynter did not look up from the bill she was studying as Bo wrung his t-shirt with agitation by her side as a rumble, nearly twice as loud as before, escaped from his throat, making the few remaining standing objects in the house, now all relocated to the floor, shake violently along with the windows. Paynter was not the girl next door anymore. Her face was drained, her eyes almost angry as she winced from the inevitable pain behind them.

'How you doing, Paynter?' I asked, recovering from my own mini-migraine. Like the noise, the pain had nearly doubled in intensity since my last visit.

She shrugged. 'I'm doing—'

'I need a snack, Mom!' her son, Mason, shouted from another room.

'It's nearly dinner. Wait!'

'I'm hungry now, Mom.'

'Wait!'

'You suck, Mom.' Footsteps on the stairs.

'Mason, get back down here! Get back down! We

do not talk to each other like that in this house!'

A bedroom door slammed.

'Do you want to go after him?'

She shook her head.

'I should do, but... what was your question?'

'Just how are you, really. All of you. But you in particular.'

'How am I? Surviving. I guess. Bills. Lots of bills. No money. Health insurance refusing to pay out. Some catch in the policy I don't understand. Savings getting eaten away. The other day I had to pay for some guy's trout, can you believe it? Bo did his thing and they leapt out of this guy's pond, which is like, several blocks away, and they died. Said he was going to sue because of the trauma of finding them dead on the ground, but I think he was just mouthing off. Hoping, anyway.'

'Other than that?'

'Other than that, the kids are going off the rails. Can't handle seeing their dad like this, so they lash out. and Bo's... well, you can see how he is. But yeah, we're all still alive.'

'If you don't mind me saying so, you look tired.'

'Yeah, I'm tired. You know how many times a day I have to go through this with him? It's near constant. At night too. I get woken up, like, four, five times, just to go through the same thing, like I've never said it before. It's...'

'Exhausting?'

'Exhausting. Frustrating. Depressing. But, hey. Death us do part. Sickness and in health. It's what I signed up for, right? No reason to complain.'

'It's only natural to complain,' I said. 'No one should have to go through what you're going through on your own.'

'Yeah. Well. No one else is stepping up. Family don't want to know. Friends I thought I could rely on won't even answer the phone. Neighbours pretend they can't even see me, except when they're shouting at me about all the headaches Bo's noise gives them…'

'It's tough,' I said, taking care to give my most empathic nod.

'Yeah, it's tough.'

Paynter cried. I would have hugged her if her husband had not been standing next to us, waving his crude, homemade costume about like a flag.

'I did not make this,' he was saying. 'I have never seen this before. I swear on the life of my firstborn I do not know what this is. So what if it's got my name in it? Anyone can write my name, can't they…'

***

'Laura. We need to go home,' I said after a silent ten minutes of thinking, back in the car, as we crossed the Bradley River Bridge.

'You're calling the hotel home? That's weird, Chas.'

'No, I mean we need to go home home. We should stop filming, take a break. Come back in two months, three.'

'Chas, we've got, like, four more things to film and then we're done. What's the point?'

'All the stories we're following already are going to get interesting if we just wait. Stuff's going to happen, but it won't happen now. We can still get this done before Christmas, if we stop now.'

'You think he's going to go Stage III, don't you?'

'Maybe, I guess, but it's not just that. It's Alex and that little gang. It's going somewhere, I can feel it.'

'Perhaps, but Jolyon isn't going to agree to financing a whole other trip on a hunch. And all the stuff we've got lined up already, I don't know if I can get them again in a few months.'

'You will. You're brilliant.'

'Well, yes, I am, but people don't like being messed around.'

'Laura, I think this could be it. This could be the big one.'

'They're not going to give us a BAFTA, Chas.'

'No, not a BAFTA. But another award, a smaller one. It won't happen though unless we follow these stories through to the end. We've got to let them grow like flowers.'

'Then cut their heads off.'

'Wasn't where I was going with that analogy, but…'

'Fine. I'll Skype Jolyon. See what I can do.'

'You're a star, Laura.'

'You're the star, Chas. I just hold the pole the star's stuck to.'

***

Laura knocked on my door later that evening. I was in a dressing gown. She was still in her jacket and boots. Ready to hit the bar, I guessed.

'Good news, Chas,' she said. 'They're shipping you out and sending you home.'

'He was OK with it?'

'No, but he acknowledges your gut instincts are good. If you think you need to wait, then that's what we'll do. I'll sort us some flights in the morning.'

'Thanks, Laura,' I said.

'No problem. Celebratory drink?'

'Nah. Read. Sleep.'

'You mean hotel porn, sleep.'

'I really don't. I'm old. And no one watches that stuff anymore.'

'Hey, remember that time you watched seven hours of the stuff and charged it to expenses?'

'No memory of that whatsoever. It must have been somebody else.'

Laura laughed.

'See you in the morning, Chas,' she said.

I closed the door and lay on the bed. Filming fraught scenes like the one at Alex's would have been a walk in a park for me just a few years ago, but now they wiped me out. Maybe because I cared more. Maybe because I was old.

I should phone Sam, I thought, and tell her I'm

coming home. But first I felt like watching some of the raw footage Laura had already uploaded to the cloud on the laptop, get a sense of what we'd done already. I watched Bo and Paynter in happier days, with him making his strange rumbling noise in the kitchen. I watched Alex at home with her parents, and all the craziness with her brother, Jim. I watched the demonstration. The little girl, Lizabeth. Wayne the butcher. Abbie and Brett simulating sex on their living room floor. Starflower out on the street. Don the Pummellor. Phoebe the escort. Theo the Rippler. Hope and her metal whip. I watched it all. And when I had, I opened some files again. Abbie and Brett. Phoebe the escort. Hope, with her catsuit open to the navel. And I lay back with my dressing gown undone and watched.

INTERLUDE

'Absolutely superb stuff, Charlie,' said Jolyon, a man secure enough in his position to talk with his mouth full. 'I didn't want to tell you at the time, and I hope you don't mind me telling you now, but before you left, I really thought this would be your last hurrah. Enthusiasm for you at the channel is waning, I'm sure you've noticed.'

I fixed a smile at this, pretending hearing it wasn't like a hammer blow. I could see Sam giving me a worried look, and reassuringly patted her hand. Laura didn't look like she was listening at all.

But with what you've got,' continued Jolyon, 'and what you've promised me you're going to get... well, I can't promise you anything, but if it does well...'

'BAFTA,' coughed Laura into her hand.

'They're not going to give you a BAFTA, Laura, you know that. But, *if* you did get one the smaller, less important awards, which is a big if, granted, that would be the first the network has ever gotten for a documentary, and only the third after that comedy prank show accidentally turned out funny in 2005. And if that happened, I can't see why they wouldn't renew your contract, on considerably more favourable terms, allowing you to make lots more lovely programmes for me.'

'I'm glad you're happy,' was all I could think to say.

'Oh, I'm very happy, Charlie. Lots of Magic Moments you've got already. One a minute, practically! This is delicious, by the way, Sam. What do you call it, again?'

'Lamprais,' said Sam. 'It's a three-meat curry and a whole load of side dishes, cooked in a banana leaf parcel. It's Sri Lankan.'

'It took all afternoon,' I said, proudly. 'It's her *pièce de résistance*.'

'Sri Lanka,' said Jolyon. 'How exotic. Is that where you're from?'

'I'm from Bromley, but my parents are Sri Lankan, yes.'

Jolyon nodded. He seemed to be having trouble with what was in his mouth, chewing it and moving it around from cheek to cheek determinedly.

'Oh, you're not meant to eat the leaf,' said Sam. 'It's just there as wrapping.'

'I see,' he muttered, and spat it out into a napkin.

It had been Sam's idea to have them over for dinner. She thought it would be good for everyone to touch base in an informal setting with a few bottles of wine, disrupting the hierarchy and make us feel like a team aiming for a shared creative goal rather than just a bunch of work colleagues. Honestly, I didn't know if it had made a difference — our lunch meetings were usually quite boozy anyway — except that Jolyon had to suffer the indignity of spitting out a masticated leaf, and we'd had to watch him do it. Still, it was a chance for Sam to shine. She was an excellent host, the food was great, and she looked beautiful in her maxi dress that looked like it would slip off her with just the lightest tug on the cord belt, revealing a seemingly naked body I knew in fact to be discreetly hoisted into place with magical undergarments.

After dessert and Irish coffee and a loose arrangement to meet up more professionally before we flew out again for Merriweather in six weeks' time, Jolyon, now sloshed enough to be telling his most outrageous industry stories, got sent home in a taxi back to the wife no one ever saw. Laura, not pissed at all despite having spent the evening drinking and saying little, I guess, so as to avoid giving too much away about herself, went back to who-knows-what. She always kept details of her private life vague. The only concrete thing I knew was that she had a son, now nearly a young man. But after living with her for much of his life, he'd decided a few years ago he wanted to live with his dad. This had freed Laura up to take lots of foreign assignments with me, something I think she did to make her mind off it all. In any case, it obviously caused Laura pain, so I never enquired further. I'd had hints of a significant other at various points who seemed to come and go, and I'd often suspected she was occasionally getting picked up, or doing the picking herself, after hours in the bar when we were on location. But whatever the situation, she seemed reasonably happy and not lonely, so it didn't bother me how she lived.

Me and Sam surveyed the washing up mountain

and decided to leave it to the morning. I had nowhere to be, anyway, so that was my day sorted. There had been a time I'd have broken the plates before doing something so mundane, but those days were long gone now.

'You did so well tonight,' I said, realising as it came out of my mouth how patronising I sounded.

'Really,' said Sam. She cocked her head to one side. 'What's my reward?'

'What do you want it to be?'

She said nothing, but pulled the cord on her dress, and it came off almost as easily as I'd imagined. I put my arms round her and kissed her, gently pushing her down onto the couch. Moving down her body, I somehow drunkenly, ridiculously ended up kissing her tummy shaping knickers.

'You're not meant to eat the wrapping,' she said, laughing, as she peeled them down.

***

We made love for the fourth time in several days. Usually we only managed it twice a week, which I knew seemed like some sexual nirvana to my friends with kids. She initiated it this time. My being away must have made her want me more, strange as it was to think that. But often it was me. I needed it, but I didn't always want it.

It wasn't so bad this time. I think the alcohol must have helped. When she went down on me on the couch, I only thought about Phoebe's tentacle tongue and what that must feel like a little bit. Her breasts escaping from her bra only vaguely reminded me of Hope and her whip hand (although it was always more the breasts than the whip that excited me still), and when she rode me, I only imagined Abbie and her elongated feet giving her that extra thrust that little bit before I came. When I cuddled her before we both fell asleep naked on the couch, I was barely thinking about rosies at all.

***

'Do you think I'm exotic?' Sam asked a couple of days later, after we'd done my morning affirmations together and just before she dressed for work. She always left early and usually came home late. Unlike me, she liked to keep busy.

'Um. I'm not sure what the right answer to that question could be,' I said, still in bed, nothing to get up for. 'Why do you ask?'

'The other day, at the dinner party. Jolyon said I was exotic.'

'He just meant he doesn't remember you from Cambridge.'

'Very funny. But is that how you think of me? Being from a different culture.'

'But you're not from a different culture, are you? You grew up watching *Thundercats* like I did.'

'Yeah, but I look different to the girls you grew up with. The food I cook is different. My family's different. I just wondered if that's how you think of me, ever, that's all.'

'I… It's never occurred to me to think along those lines, honestly. Maybe because I've seen so much weird stuff. Someone knowing how to cook with a banana leaf, it's… nothing, really.'

'You don't see me as the Other?'

'Only in the sense you've got a fanny.'

'Christ, you're such a little boy, sometimes,' she said, and hit me playfully and hard enough to hurt.

***

Of course, I'd been lying. My relationship with Sam was built around total honesty, but there had to be limits. I had thought of her as exotic, even if I didn't see it in those terms, when I'd met her. She came from a big family who loved her. She cooked so well because her mum and her aunties had taken time to teach her. Sam's natural instinct, as well as that as all her family, was to see the good in people, while I made my living wheedling out the bad and laughing at it. She looked after herself, exercising, drinking rarely and never doing drugs, despite working in an industry that was a cocaine blizzard at the time. I suspected she was also quietly religious, one of several sisters who would accompany their ageing mother to church on a rota basis, although she kept it so much to herself it never came up as an issue. No, to me, Sam wasn't just exotic. She was from a different planet.

And now I lived on that planet. Exotic was the new normal. Maybe I needed a new exotic. Maybe that's why as soon as she left, I was scrolling through streaming videos tagged 'Rosie', watching girls with tongues like Phoebe's working their magic on headless men's cocks, or men with dicks like Don's seemingly take young women to a level no other dick could let them reach. Rosies whose anus had been replaced by something alien and malleable. And just rosies fucking. Naked fucking rosies. Rosies in costume. Rosies with wings, rosies with shells, rosies with hooves. Rosies with tails that went where they shouldn't, rosies with claws that scratched backs and drew blood. Every type of rosie, it seemed, from all over the world, sucking, screwing, coming.

It had been like this every day since I got back. Sam would go to work, I would watch this shit. I felt stupid afterwards, and guilty. Not because it was porn. Sam knew that I watched it, and I think she did herself, once a month, when she had a spare five minutes. But because for the first time, I was wanting something she couldn't provide.

Every so often I'd try and go cold turkey and distract myself with some actual work. I'd pop into the office and brainstorm ideas for future programmes with researchers, although there was nothing I could get excited about. After all, what was there left, after rosies? I'd meet up with the few old friends I could still deal with now I wasn't on something. Cinema in the afternoon. A visit from my brother who, after his suicide attempt, became a Buddhist and now lived a life of abstinence so strict it put my own sedate state to shame. Obviously we'd spent the entire afternoon stepping around all the family history that directly led to his near-death experience and indirectly to my assorted issues.

The need to break the pattern got so strong that I nearly accepted an invitation to a showbiz party from an old colleague who had gone on to things much bigger than my silly programmes. For a second, I entertained the thought that a return to my old habit would be preferable to my new one. Then reality kicked in and I firmly clicked 'will not be attending' in the little box.

Even when I wasn't watching it, I was thinking about it. If I saw a rosie in the street I'd wonder how they did it and, if it was a woman, what it would be like to do it with them. And then I'd go home and have sex with Sam that evening, if she wasn't too tired, thinking about that woman on the street. It wasn't that I didn't want Sam. It's just that I wanted nearly everything else, every possible marvellous new variation on human that the rosie world made possible as well. Sam was beginning to wonder what was going on with my libido. Was it something I was eating?

I hated having a secret life I hid from her. It felt unnatural, against the natural order of my everyday wellbeing. She was the person I could share everything with, but I couldn't share this.

Meanwhile, Laura would message me with developments in Merriweather. Bo had spent the last of their savings on a costume from HEROSsories. Alex wasn't returning her calls. While I began to hate the behavioural loop I'd got stuck in, I also came to dread going back. Something was going to happen. I was going to have sex with a rosie and destroy my relationship with Sam, I knew it. Even though I didn't want a single thing in my life to change, and all I had to do to avoid it was simply not do it, the thought that I was going to do precisely this thing wouldn't leave me. I didn't understand it, and maybe because of that it wouldn't let me go, coming at me with the inevitability of a speeding truck.

And one day, I wasn't in the flat anymore with Sam. I was on a plane, crossing the Atlantic, going back to Merriweather, fearing our landing. Fearing the impact. Fearing everything falling apart.

STAGE III

HEROS
UNBOUND

'Hi, Chad, how you doing?' Bo shook my hand enthusiastically as we stepped through the door, a wide beaming smile on his face. The agitated neurotic of a couple of months ago was nowhere to be seen. This Bo exuded joy and wellbeing, not just back to his old self, but more so.

'I'm OK, Bo,' I said. 'How are you? You look a lot better than last time we saw you.'

'I'm great. Yeah, I had a bit of, I dunno, a bug or something for a while, but that's all done with now. Moved past that. Now I'm back on my feet, living my best life, raring to go.'

'Yeah, I can see that,' I said. I spotted Paynter in a doorway, shovelling peanut and jelly sandwiches into a child.

'Hi, Paynter,' I said, going in for a hug. 'How's it going?'

She smiled a little smile as I squeezed her. She looked like she hadn't slept for a long time. She answered, 'Better. I guess. I dunno. Is this better?'

'Well, it seems better,' I said. 'Bo looks and sounds a lot better.'

'Give it five minutes,' she said. 'You'll see what the problem is.'

'Hey, Mason!' shouted Bo to his son, hovering behind his mother. 'Do you wanna show Chad how we Americans play football, huh? Not soccer, but American football! Score some touchdowns out in the yard, huh?'

Mason looked at him uncertainly, as if he couldn't quite process this new version of his dad, that there was almost too much of him. 'I don't know, Dad,' he said. 'Maybe later.'

'Let's do it now, Mason. Throw the ball around. Show this limey how it's done.'

'Maybe later,' said Mason, and disappeared into the kitchen.

A look of confusion and disappointment fell over Bo's face.

'I just gotta… go upstairs and do something,' he said.

I watched him go, walking almost as if in a dream.

'Listen,' said Paynter. 'You'll hear him opening the closet.'

Sure enough, there was the faint creak of a wardrobe door, opening and closing.

'Now,' said Paynter. 'Give it two minutes, you'll hear the window.'

'Two minutes. That's quite quick.'

'It is, but he's getting faster. The doctor said he'll

have it down to one minute within a week.'

'Are there any safety precautions you can take?'

'I put up a ladder.'

'A ladder?'

'Yeah, if he sees the ladder he might go for it. He still tries to do the tree a lot though, which is scary.'

'I can imagine.'

As Paynter predicted, there was the sound of a window opening.

'Could you not just lock it shut?'

'If I did that, he would break the window. Once the pattern's been set, you can't really change it. You want to see what he does? Come this way, look out the kitchen window.'

I followed Paynter to the kitchen. The kitchen window was open, and I could put my head out easily. Laura slipped out the back door to film.

'I can't watch anymore,' said Paynter. 'Is he on the ladder?'

I looked up. Bo was not on the ladder.

'No,' I said. 'He's in the tree.'

'Oh god.'

I watched as Bo, in his new costume from HER-OSsories, with sculpted trout head and silvery bodysuit that shimmered with a rainbow of colour when it caught the light, swung from the branches from the high tree in the yard, hanging precariously as he worked his way down, before finally hitting the trunk and dropping to the ground.

'One day he's going to fall,' said Paynter. 'He'll break his back and that will be it.'

Bo ran, fast, like an athlete, out the yard and onto the road with no sidewalk, his rumble, now strangely proud and resplendent, like a cockerel's comb, rattling the pans of the kitchens of the streets as he passed them.

'Where is he going?' I asked, the pain that wrapped from behind my eyes to the back of the skull at last subsiding.

'Wherever he thinks there's crime,' said Paynter. 'And that could be… anywhere.'

***

Several hours after returning to Merriweather, my head was emptied of all thoughts of sex with anybody as we did the rounds, re-establishing relationships with our interviewees, picking up new leads and making plans. The thrill of the chase, the satisfaction of a job competently done — these took over completely, leaving my old obsession seem simply bizarre. I felt so stupid, letting the idea snowball in my head and ruin the past few months of my life when I could have been guiltlessly enjoying my time at home with Sam.

It was autumn now in Merriweather, a notably sublime experience in this part of the country. The leaves on the trees and ground were a cascade of yellows, oranges, and reds that left the British autumn I escaped looking dull and brown in comparison. There was a pinch in the air that made me think of the beginnings of new school terms and fresh possibilities. New starts, new stages. I felt quietly elated as we crossed the Bradly River Bridge again, looking down on the ribbon of trees that ran alongside the river's left bank, and for the moment couldn't see how anything could stop me from feeling that way.

***

'So, Dr. Wexler, what happens when a HEROSic person enters Stage III?'

Dr. Wexler sighed and psyched herself up to answer my stupid question. Her office smelt of fresh bread.

'When they progress to Stage III, instead of suffering acute anxiety over their split identity as in Stage II, they instead enter a state of seeming unawareness. They will go about their daily lives as if the costumed self does not exist, often becoming an exaggerated version of their pre-HEROS identity. Just the tiniest agitation, however, can cause their sense of self to fracture, and they then withdraw into their costumed identity.'

'And they fight crime. Or try to.'

'Wow. You've actually read something before coming to talk to me this time. Well done. Yes. They attempt to fight crime until they feel they have thwarted a sufficient amount of it, at which point they revert to their everyday self.'

'Are you making bread?'

'What makes you ask that?'

'The smell of bread.'

Dr. Wexler paused, as if wondering whether to trust me with sacred knowledge.

'Yes, I have a bread maker. It does baguettes.'

'Can we try one?

'Why?'

'It would be good for the programme.'

'No, you cannot.'

***

'Can we use any of that?' I asked Laura as we crossed back over the Bradley River Bridge, the autumnal riot of colour below mocking my newly flat mood.

'Not really.'

'You're going to use it, aren't you?'

'Yep.'

***

Although perhaps no longer ecstatic, I was still keen to explore the world of Stage III HEROS. First, however, I wanted to see if I could track Alex down. Laura had been unable to get her to answer any calls or emails in the UK, and she still wasn't picking up now. A call to her parents' house had led to a brisk answer of 'we cannot help you' and the phone being put down by her father. We decided to head straight for her hostel.

Janvier, the young French-Canadian whose

'sparking' resulted in him regularly catching alight and his sleeping on fireproof sheets, opened the door for us. I asked him if Alex was still living there.

He shook his head.

Did he know where she had gone, I asked.

He shook his head again and looked at the floor. He knew something, but he wasn't going to tell us.

I thanked him and we went on our way.

***

We phoned Abbie. I dared myself to think about how many times I'd fantasised about her sexually over the past few weeks. But the thoughts did not want to come, almost as if they resented even being summoned. She answered quickly and the door closed on them with some finality.

'Hi, Charlie! You're back!' she cried, sounding genuinely pleased to hear from me.

'Hi, Abbie!' I said. 'How's it going?'

'Very well, thank you. Are you going to stop by again? Brett and I would love to have you.'

'That's a very kind offer I may take you up on. But right now, I'm trying to find Alex. Do you know where she is?'

'Oh, OK.' She sounded deflated. 'I don't really hang out with that crowd anymore. It was all getting very extreme, very, what's the word...'

'Militant?'

'Yeah. Militant. So, anyway, I'm not the person to

ask.'

'It's just that she doesn't seem to be living at the hostel anymore, and she's not answering voice-mails or emails.'

'Oh, right. Have you tried her family? I understand they live locally.'

'They don't want to talk to us. Last time we saw them, things didn't go well, from their perspective.'

'I can't help you, I don't think... wait. You say she's not answering her phone or emails?'

'That's right.'

'Then she may have gone off-grid. And if she's done that... yeah, I have an idea about where she might be.'

And Abbie told us of a place even Laura had not uncovered in her research. A place that few but rosies knew about, and almost none but rosies had ever visited. I didn't even need to look at her to know Laura was smiling at the very thought of the challenge.

HEROS IN ISOLATION

Rosetown sits about twenty miles outside of Merriweather, hidden in thick woodland. An isolationist community made up entirely of HEROSic people, it is incredibly difficult to find or even make contact with. There is just one phone in Rosetown, an old flip-top mobile that sits on a desk in the main building, used for contacting emergency services when necessary. The number of this phone is closely protected, and is shared between rosies on the outside only with great secrecy and caution. It took Laura a full three hours to find it which, for her, is very slow.

The first time we phoned, they hung up on us immediately. It was only after we phoned two more times and mentioned the names of the rosies who provided us with the number that the voice on the end, gruff and guarded, and for reasons I didn't fully understand however glad I was of them, reluctantly agreed to our making a very brief visit. There was just one condition. Thanks to Laura's miraculous skills of persuasion, they would let us film — the first time this had ever happened in Rosetown — but only when they said so. They would dictate entirely when the camera went on and off. This was against our values as documentarians, at least the few Laura and me could agree on, but we accepted it. We were the first outsiders ever to be let in and film the place. Sometimes you just don't get to quibble with destiny.

We had been told to wait in a clearing by the roadside. You would have no idea anyone lived anywhere near the spot. Even though we couldn't see them, however, they must have been able to see us, because eventually a man with grey, rock-like skin and carrying a rifle appeared from out of the trees, still only barely visible in his camouflage gear.

'This way,' he said, and led us down what might loosely be described as a path into the woods. It was quite dramatic and mysterious, and I was annoyed Laura wasn't filming, but there was no way round that. Not giving any hint of their location was one of the rules that we had promised to abide by.

'Is it a long way?' I said, trying to get some conversation going with the unsmiling man who resembled a cliff face.

'It's as long as it is,' he said, without a smile, although I'm not sure that he could if he'd wanted to.

'Are you the person we spoke to on the phone?' I asked. But he said nothing more. It was clear our conversation was over.

There was a new smell in the air. Something like school dinners. A glint of sun on something. And the wood was suddenly behind us and there stood Rosetown.

To be honest, it was a bit grim at first sight, on that cold, drizzly autumn day. Essentially a series of Portakabins on the side of a hill, plus what looked and smelt like a pig sty. But when you looked more closely, you could see that up in the trees, between the Portakabins, were wooden structures in a style that I hadn't seen anywhere else before. Curved, bulbous things with circular entrances from which rope ladders hung down, they seemed ingeniously constructed and quite beautiful.

There didn't seem to be anyone about, and it was all quite silent, until a child screamed joyfully and I saw a play park beyond the Portakabins. A small boy flew down a slide and into a bed of woodchip, re-emerging to carry out the happy action all over again. When I turned back to the huts, there were a number of people in front of me — men and women, from young to old, all apparently rosies — all wearing similar camouflage gear to the rock-faced man, and despite some having replacement organs that looked lethal, nevertheless all were carrying a weapon of some kind, from a simple knife to a semiautomatic.

An old man with a beard passed through them and stood before us. He looked somewhat Old Testament, and his eyes stared straight through you, as if you were standing in the way of God. He alone did not appear to be armed. Whatever replacement organ he possessed, it was hidden from sight.

'Well,' he said. And nothing else.

'Are you the person we spoke to on the phone?' I asked.

'I guess I was,' he said.

'Are you in charge here?' I said.

'They seem to think I am,' he said, gesturing to all who surrounded him.

'Can I ask what your name is?'

'You can ask.' There was a little smile at the side of his mouth as a ripple of laughter went around. He was playing with us a bit, for his own amusement, and maybe everyone else's.

'So... what's your name?'

'Steve,' he said. I have to say, I was expecting something with more gravitas.

'I'm Charlie,' I said. 'And this is Laura.'

He shrugged. It obviously didn't matter what our names were. He had no use for them.

'Is there somewhere we can go and chat?' I said. 'Turn the camera on, get you explaining what you're trying to do here?'

'We can go to the dining hall. It's lunchtime.'

'That sounds superb. Where is it?'

'You're standing on it.'

I saw now that there was a funnel emerging out of the earth from which steam and the school dinner smell was coming from.

177

'You've hollowed out the hill?'

'In case of attack,' he said. 'When we're in lock-down, it's impenetrable.'

'Why would anyone attack this place?'

He rolled his eyes.

'Don't you know your history, boy? Ruby Ridge. Waco. You set yourself apart. You have guns for your own protection. One day, they attack.'

'So why don't you just not set yourself apart and not have guns?'

'Well we could do that,' he said, dryly. 'And we could just wait for us to be taken out, one by one, on the streets.'

I wondered if he knew about the force field that formed around a group of rosies when under attack. But as he looked straight through me again, his eyes bulging at some potential apocalypse going on behind me, I thought that this was maybe a man who simply enjoyed hollowing out hills and hiding in them.

'Maybe we should get some lunch,' I said, trying to break the silence that his stare necessitated.

'Why, what you brought with you?' he said. 'Just kidding. We always have leftovers.'

With that, he led us down the hill, and through an opening in the ground. It had the thickest doors I'd ever seen, ready to slam shut at the first sign of attack.

***

It looked like the whole population of Rosetown had gathered in the dining hall. Nearly a hundred in all, the sound of their cutlery and chairs scraping echoed deafeningly off the metal walls and ceiling. They weren't letting us film here either. Each rosie would have to be approached individually for permission. Most of them didn't want to be found by the people they had once ran away from. And as servers ladled nearly grey stew spotted with the tiniest bits of what might have been ham into bowls that we carried on our school cafeteria trays back to one of several long tables, I kept an eye out for Alex.

Our sources said that she had been saying she was heading here six weeks ago. The question was, did she just pass through, or was she still here, if she ever arrived at all? Although Rosetown was closed to the outside world, rosies were generally welcome to use it as a place of respite, if they could handle the peculiar lifestyle. But now was not the time to ask about Alex. Right now we simply had to convince them that we were sincere and trustworthy, something that would prove to be a challenge considering the inherently paranoid mindset of the place.

Steve gestured to us to sit down opposite him. As he slurped his grey stew, he told us about how they had reached virtual self-sufficiency at Rosetown, with solar and wind-generated electricity, growing their own crops and rearing animals. They had achieved so much, he was saying, not only because of some rosies' physical superiority, but because he believed that rosies were mentally and socially superior to the rest of us. I had seen no evidence for this (the stew was certainly no evidence of any superiority), and would have said so, but I was distracted. I could see, down the other end of the hall, Kenzie — the winged rosie who had been at Alex's hostel both times we had been there. I couldn't see Alex, but there was no way her being at Rosetown wasn't connected to her in some way.

'Sorry, am I boring you, young man?' said Steve, realising my attention was elsewhere.

'I'll be right back,' I said, vaguely, and sprang down the hall in the direction of Kenzie. I had barely made it a quarter of the way there when there were several clicks. Rifles were pointing at me from every direction. I stopped moving.

'I… I just saw someone I know,' I said.

Slowly, the rifles lowered. I turned to see Steve glaring from the bench. I wondered if he had some kind of psychic connection with or even control of the other residents of Rosetown.

'Don't do that again,' he said, and went back to slurping his stew.

I walked back to my seat. It took a while for me to summon up the courage to glance down the hall again, but when I did, Kenzie was no longer there.

***

'The treehouses are living spaces for families. Everyone else is in the dorms.'

Steve had seemed to have forgiven me and was showing me around Rosetown, while Laura was allowed to film. I still had the nagging sense he might be able to read my mind.

'Are you in a treehouse or in a dorm?'

'Hey, you're really tricky, you know that, Charlie? In answer to your question, I do have a treehouse because I need space to plan and work, although I occupy it alone.'

'You don't have a family?'

'I didn't say that.'

'So your family is…'

'Somewhere else, and that's all I'm saying.'

'Not here? Out in the world outside?'

'Somewhere else, Charlie.'

There were several Portakabins at the bottom of the hill, set apart from the rest of Rosetown. I was pretty certain I could also see someone attempting to climb out of a window.

'What are those down there?' I asked.

'That's where we look after those of us who go on to Stages II and III. They're well cared for, much better than they would be outside, because we understand their needs.'

'And do you have a place for caring for those at Stage IV?'

'Ain't no helping them when they get to that,' he said, and gazed into the woods. A breeze blew threw the trees, followed by an unnerving still-ness.

***

The tour was over. Steve had shown us everything he was going to, and we sat in his treehouse study. It was quite spare, save for some hard chairs, a naïve painting of Niagara Falls, and a desk with an ancient word processor and printer loaded with computer paper on it and an old flip-top phone in the centre.

'Very cosy,' I said.

'Cosy enough for me,' he said.

'You don't have any photographs. Of your family.'

'Don't need them. They're all up here,' he gestured to his temple.

'Do you have a photographic memory?'

'Cute, Charlie. No, I just have a normal memory. But I'm not telling you about my family.'

'Painful?'

'You can draw your own conclusions.'

'From…?'

He gestured round the room and then out the window.

'I don't follow.'

'Christ, Charlie,' he snapped, standing up to pace as he spoke. 'Are all the physiotypicals as dumb as you? I'm in pain. They're in pain. We're all in pain. We've isolated ourselves in the middle of the damn woods because everything out there, in the big wide world, causes us pain. So, yeah, if my family's out there, and I'm in here, it's a source of pain to me.'

'But is hiding yourself away a solution?' I asked. 'Surely it would be better to work towards better integration and understanding of rosies in the larger world, not to remove them from it out of sight?'

He shook his head and gazed out the circular window.

'Don't you think I tried? Don't you think we all tried, in our way? Maybe not on a big scale, but in our own little pocket of life? We're all here because we're tired, Charlie. We're all so tired of fighting. We'd rather put our energies into building something new, not try and turn the tide. Sometimes… you just need a place you can rest.'

'I know the feeling.'

'I very much doubt that.'

I had no more questions except the big one.

'Um, as well as wanting to explore your wonderful community, we are also here because we are trying to find a rosie we were documenting earlier in the year, and we had heard she had come here. Her name was Alex, and if I were to show you her photo, would you be able to tell me if she passed through here, or if indeed she is still here?'

I reached for the photo I had hidden in my jacket, but Steve waved it away.

'You don't need to show me any photo. I'm not going to help you find anybody here. If they're here, and they want to be found, they'll let you know.'

'Could you not just look at the photograph?'

'Are you deaf?'

He glared through me again, and as he did so, I wondered once more about who this guy was, what situation he had left behind to come here. I realised we would probably never know. But perhaps there was something he could tell us.

'OK, Steve, changing the subject. Would you be able to tell us what organ replacement you have? I was thinking that maybe there was something in your brain that gave you mind control. You seem to be able to control everyone round here very well.'

He stopped glaring and laughed.

'No, no mind control here. They're just very well drilled. Like I said, we are essentially superior. No, my difference is my heart.'

'Your heart? A heart organ replacement is very rare.'

'Yes, it's only happened a few times worldwide. Not many people survive it.'

'So, what does your heart… do, exactly?'

His eyes began to see through me again. I thought I was going to be shouted at for some reason. But then he closed them, as if making a decision.

'It glows. You can see it through my flesh.'

'Like E.T.'s?'

'I guess so. I don't really know that movie.'

'That sounds quite manageable. Quite sweet, almost. I don't see why you would need to hide yourself away up here over that.'

'It doesn't glow all the time.'

'No. It's not glowing now. When does it glow?'

He took a deep breath.

'It glows… when I lie.'

'And did you lie to your family?'

He nodded.

'Was it about something bad?'

He nodded again. I could see that he was crying.

'Maybe they'll see this and know that I'm sorry,' he said, softly, and I realised why he had perhaps agreed to let us film in the first place.

We said our goodbyes and made our way down the rope ladder soon after.

**

We stood, waiting for the rock-faced man to reappear and guide us back to the car. Meanwhile, I looked around at Rosetown, watched as rosies came and went quietly between the Portakabins, living a life of almost mechanical utility, always camouflage-clad and with a weapon on their person. Perhaps this was the way it needed to be, to keep working the machine for living that they had made, looking to the smallest gesture of Steve's for guidance. It may be necessary, I thought, but no one seemed that free.

'Charlie! Hey, it's me! Kenzie!'

Kenzie came running from a Portakabin, her small wings flapping fruitlessly behind her. Like everyone else, she was wearing the camouflage trousers and shirt, but she looked more ill-suited to it than the rest, as if dressed for a fancy-dress party she wanted to leave.

'Hey, I saw you earlier!' I called to her. 'How come you're here?'

'Oh,' she said as she reached us, 'just needed to get away from things for a bit. It gets you down, you know, out there sometimes.'

'Is it better here?'

'Well, the food's not!'

'Not a stew fan, huh?'

'No, and it is kinda like a cult with these stupid clothes, or a summer camp. And there isn't anything that fun to do. But you know what's good? You're invisible. No one's looking at you at all. Whether you've got wings, scales, whatever, no one is even thinking about it. No one's marking you out as one of *those*, and making a decision not to let you do something, or have something, because of that. And you know what? It is so good not to have that, just for a bit.'

She began to cry as she spoke. They were tears of relief.

I didn't want to change the subject. She was giving us some good footage. But I had to. The rock-face man was coming and our time was nearly up.

'Did you come here with Alex?'

She smiled, as if she always knew this was really

about her friend.

'Yeah, but she didn't last long. Doing what she's told ain't exactly her style. Her and Steve fell out big time. He thought she was trying to take over.'

'Was she?'

'Yeah, well, maybe a little bit. But only over small things like the clothes. Bit of a rebellion, there.'

'She wouldn't wear the camo? I thought she liked combats.'

'She is very particular. Apparently, her gear did not match the foliage round here.'

'That's a pretty niche point of contention.'

'Yeah, well, it's Alex, so…'

'Why did she come here?'

'I think this was just her way of clearing her head. Getting a fresh outlook.'

'A reboot.'

'Yeah, a reboot. For the future.'

'Why, what's she planning?'

'You'd have to ask her that.'

'I'd love to. Do you know where she is?'

Kenzie looked around cagily.

'If Alex wants to talk to you, she'll find you.'

'Can you tell her I'm looking for her, next time you see her?'

'Oh, she'll know already.'

I thought I could get a little more from her if I pressed her, but it was too late. The rock-faced man had reached us. Kenzie gave us a little wave as he gestured to the woods with his rifle. I took one last look at Rosetown. And just before we entered the trees blocked my view for good, I saw them. In the far distance, beyond the Portakabins for the later stages, a couple of short rows of wooden crosses. This town was so self-sufficient, it had its own graveyard. I was surprised, then wondered why I was surprised. What else were they to do, once the inevitable happened? The woods felt heavy as we walked through, and I was glad to see the car through the trees.

HEROS AT LARGE

'You know what's so dumb about all this crimefighting crap? None of it makes any sense, that's what. Look at me. I combat crime. It's my job. On me right now, I have a firearm. Taser. Pepper spray. Handcuffs. These are all things that are proven to be effective when dealing with perpetrators. That's why we use 'em. But look at this guy, walking down the street now. He's got, what, coming out of his hands? They're like, paper streamers or something? What possible good could they be in stopping and apprehending someone involved in a criminal act? Nine times out of ten, whatever weird thing your body is now doing is not going to help you apprehend a criminal. You gotta leave it to us. But there's no telling them that. It's all so dumb. D.U.M.B. Dumb.'

Patrol Officer Paul Frankopan was driving me down Main Street. This was a location to which those Stage IIIs gravitated, looking for crime to fight in their costumes. At this time of night, it was not unusual to see a crimefighter every fifty yards or so. HEROSsories adverts were on every bus shelter.

'I'll tell you what else is dumb,' continued Officer Frankopan. 'Capes. They all wear capes. Real long ones mostly. How is that going to help you when faced with an active, possibly violent criminal? It can get caught on something, you can trip up on it, it limits your arm movement. They don't think it through. At all.'

'But it's all part of an illness,' I said to him. 'It's a series of compulsions. Rational thought doesn't really come to it.'

'Yeah, I keep on having to remind myself of that,' he said, turning the corner into a side street where there had been reports of a commotion. 'I feel sorry for them, I really do. But dealing with the dumbness of it all is practically my life now. No one actually commits a crime like armed robbery anymore, because they don't want to deal with someone waving their streamer hands in their face when they do. Because it's just another person they've got to decide on whether to take a risk on shooting or not.'

'So in a way they're very effective.'

'In a way, yeah. When they're not getting shot.'

It was all quiet now. Two people were waiting. Staff from a pizza place in their peaked paper hats, standing out the back. They were surrounded by pizzas that had fallen out of their boxes, and now lay collecting dirt on the sidewalk.

'OK, guys, what happened?' asked Officer Frankopan.

'We were just loading up the delivery van, about

half an hour ago,' one of them replied. 'We had, like, a big order, college kids having a party or something. And then, this guy, a rosie, he's just suddenly there, hanging upside down from that lamppost, there.'

'He was hanging from his feet,' said the other, 'which were like suction pads, you know?'

'Was he wearing a costume?' asked Officer Frankopan.

'Oh yeah. He looked like a frog. All white, and like a frog mask on, with big red eyes on the top of his head.'

'Was he wearing a cape?'

'No, he wasn't. Just frog stuff.'

'OK, then what happened?'

'And then he goes, give back the pizzas,' said the first, 'and we were like, excuse me, and he was saying some crazy shit about how we were part of some gang, that we were just dressed like we work here and how we're really stealing the pizzas...'

'Yeah, he said we work for someone called King Chameleon...'

Officer Frankopan sighed, as if that was significant, but tiresome.

'And that was when he grabbed a big pile of pizzas I was carrying...'

'And we were like, hey, get off them, you nut...'

'And he keeps on trying to get them off me...'

'And he was still upside-down, attached to the lamppost with his feet, at this point?' asked Officer Frankopan.

'Yeah, he was. So he's pulling, I'm pulling…'

'And I grab onto him and help him pull…'

'And that's when the pizzas end up on the ground. And that's like, a lot of pizza. A hundred dollars' worth, easy.'

'Yeah, and that guy, I guess he thought that was a job well done, because he's like, tell King Chameleon I beat you, and he's up that lamppost and then he just kinda… leaps away.'

'OK,' said Officer Frankopan. 'I think I know who this guy is. I'll try and track him down. You got HEROS insurance?'

The men nodded. Businesses in Merriweather often took out special insurance to protect them from losses caused by the activities of Stage IIIs, their adverts vying for billboard space with HEROSsories across Merriweather. As it was necessary to call the police and receive a crime number in order to claim, much of Officer Frankopan's work involved investigating these minor incidents.

Officer Frankopan took a few more details and left the men to clear up their pizzas.

***

'You sighed when they mentioned King Chameleon,' I asked, once we were back in the car.

'Man, I am so sick of hearing about King Chameleon,' said Officer Frankopan.

'Why?'

'Because there is no King Chameleon. He's just

this urban legend that gets passed around between rosies. They think he's this Mr. Big who controls all the crime in Merriweather. And he's got minions everywhere who are in disguise. But the people they think are in disguise are just actual people going about their business. Every so often it dies down and you think it's over, but then it flares up again. And it creates so many incidents, I'm sick of hearing about it.'

'You're *sure* there's no King Chameleon?'

'Well, if he is, he's disguised himself so well he hasn't left a single shred of his existence, so I'm saying no.'

Just then, I saw a figure clinging to the side of a wall.

'Hey! Is that the person we're looking for up there?'

'Nah,' said Officer Frankopan. 'That's The Stretched Sloth. We're looking for Ghost Frog.'

'The Stretched Sloth?'

'Yeah. Look at her arms. They stretch out long, like a sloth's. And she's got kinda grappling hook hands. And she's really slow.'

I looked harder. I could see what the police officer described. This rosie was just about identifiable as female through her layer of fur-covered Hidron, somewhat pear-shaped, and indeed very slow.

'But this comes back to my earlier point,' said Officer Frankopan. 'She's out here, putting herself at risk, trying to fight crime by moving very slowly across the side of a building. How is that helping anybody?'

'She can't help it,' I reminded him. 'It's a compulsion.'

'I know, I know,' he said, dismissively. 'It's just you see it every day and it wears you down, even if you understand it.'

I was struck by the duality of Officer Frankopan's attitude to the Stage IIIs. Working with them and knowing their ways intimately, but also finding them annoying. There were obviously things he wanted to get off his chest.

'You know,' he continued, unable to leave The Stretched Sloth behind, even though she was now a block behind us, 'I could arrest her right now for trespassing. Being stuck to the side of a building is just as illegal as breaking into it.'

'Why don't you?'

'The Facility's full already tonight. It gets full every night. I'd have to have a really good reason for sending someone there.'

'Is the police overstretched generally over this?'

'You bet. This patrol is a two-man job, no question. But I'm here all on my lonesome. All those kids saying 'Defund the Police' should take a ride with me. If I go down, I go down, and there ain't no one to save my ass.'

'Has any Stage III ever posed a significant threat to you?'

'Not yet. But there's always a first time.'

Officer Frankopan directed my attention to a group of Stage IIIs on a street corner.

'Look,' he said. 'They're gathering. Exchanging information. Well, what they think is information. This is how the idea of King Chameleon spreads.'

'Like a virus.'

'Exactly. I'm gonna stop and go talk to them.'

He pulled up nearby and we approached them. A mix of men and women, they looked around nervously, like startled meerkats. For a split second, I thought one of them, wearing a fish-themed costume, might be Bo. I'd promised Paynter I'd keep an eye out for him. But so far, The Trout had stayed resolutely in his suburban stomping ground, kept busy with tiny fake crime scenes left by HEROS Support for him to find, complete with volunteer perpetrators he can apprehend, and this was a different species of fish before me.

'Hey, any of you seen Ghost Frog?' Officer Frankopan asked them.

They all shook their heads emphatically and muttered that they hadn't.

'If you see him, tell him I'm looking for him, OK? Now, what you guys discussing here? You're not saying anything about King Chameleon, are you? I don't want to hear any of that talk round here.'

All of them looked at the ground noncommittedly and shuffled.

'Now, you people take care, hear? Stay out of trouble, go home when you can.'

With a sigh of resignation, Officer Frankopan left them to their own devices and we headed back to the patrol car. The sound of their whispered babble sprung up behind us. I was pretty sure I heard them say something about 'crisis actor pizza guys'.

'What is their relationship with the police?' I asked, back in the vehicle. 'Are they co-operative or…?'

'It's complicated,' said Officer Frankopan. 'On the one hand, they look to us, because they're crimefighters, right? They believe in maintaining law and order and that's what we the Police are about. On the other, they believe absolutely that it is their place in the world to tackle crime themselves. So if we get in the way of that, they will fight back. Or try to.'

'Do you think they were lying just now about not having seen Ghost Frog? They didn't look like they were telling the truth to me.'

'Probably not,' he said, opening the car door. 'They are generally supportive of each other's efforts. It's rare to see a confrontation between Stage IIIs, unless they've gone Negative. So, yeah, they were probably covering for him. He's been this — wait, I see him!'

There, crouched improbably on a protruding neon shop sign, was a man in a bright white frog costume, his suction cup feet holding him in position. Officer Frankopan stopped the car with a screech.

'Hey! You!' he shouted, jumping out and reaching for his weapon which, from a British perspective, seemed quite extreme in a crime situation where the main victims were pizzas. 'Police! Get down now!'

Ghost Frog bent his legs and sprung. His leap took him across the street and onto the roof of a parked van. The police officer altered course and aimed his weapon.

'Get down! Off the van! Onto the ground! Now!'

The man in the frog costume prepared to leap again. This time his frog's legs took him back across the street and into an alleyway, where there was a loud clank and a thud.

Officer Frankopan ran back across the road. Me and Laura followed, trying not to get hit by traffic.

'What's happened?' I cried into the alleyway.

Officer Frankopan stood over a decked Ghost Frog.

'He hit a fire escape,' he said. 'Not sure how bad he's hurt.'

Officer Frankopan called for back-up and an ambulance. I looked at Ghost Frog. There was a large dent in his mask, and he was clutching his left leg, blood soaking the white Hidron. He groaned mournfully at his fate.

'So what are you going to do?' I asked.

'Arrest him. Have him taken back to the station, depending on his medical situation. Once he's been processed, he can spend the night in the Facility if they have room, in the cells if not.'

'His medical situation looks pretty bad.'

'Well, it's not up to me to say.'

Ghost Frog carried on groaning. Remarkably, he turned over, putting all his weight on his good leg, and tried to stand up.

'Get down on the ground!' shouted Officer Frankopan, pulling a device that looked almost like some sort of electric carving fork from its holster.

Finding he couldn't rise, the crimefighter began to drag himself in the opposite direction, very slowly, his suction cup feet flopping hopelessly behind him. A red dot appeared on the white of his good leg.

'Stop or I will fire!'

Like an automaton unable to stop attempting to carry out its function, Ghost Frog just kept on dragging himself through the dirt of the alleyway.

'Warned you, bud.'

Officer Frankopan fired the device. Darts landed in the crawling man's leg and he jerked with pain as electricity surged through him. I was grimly reminded of school experiments with electricity and frog's legs.

'Oh, god,' I said, watching him writhe until the electricity cut out. 'That's not a normal taser gun is it?'

'No, it is not. We need extra-long and extra-sharp darts to puncture that material those jerks at HEROSsories make their costumes from.'

'He really looks like he's in pain now.'

'Shouldn't have tried to run.'

The dark alley became that bit darker for a moment, as if something had come in-between us and the light from the streetlamp outside. I thought I heard some sort of swoosh above, like a kite in the wind. I looked up. There was nothing there.

And then something round and hard hit Officer Frankopan right on the back of the head. He fell to the ground with a thump.

Footsteps came towards us. Movement in the shadows told me were already surrounded. Not just behind and in front, but also from above.

'Should have let him run, Officer,' said a voice. A flame lit up the alleyway, a steady branch of fire rising up from someone's hand. A group of at least five rosies, all clad in sleek black outfits, their faces fully covered except for the eyes. And no capes. This was not HEROSsories's work. This was tasteful.

While two of the group gently lifted Ghost Frog up from the ground, another advanced towards us. The leader, you could tell. Small in stature, but oozing authority.

'We will not permit the persecution of rosies,' the leader said, looking down at Officer Frankopan, barely conscious on the ground. Although their voice was muffled by the mask, it sounded like a woman. I stepped forward, but something like an arm, but probably not, held me back. Glancing at Laura, whose way was similarly blocked by some barely describable limb, but who nevertheless continued filming, I could see that neither of us stood a chance of successfully intervening.

'For the crime of violence towards one of our kind,' intoned their leader, 'I sentence you to...

erasure!'

Reaching down, the leader pulled off one glove. She put her hand on Officer Frankopan's head, his eyes trying to focus on this dark figure before him, as he tried to form words.

'I'm a police officer,' I thought I heard him croak. 'Stand ba…'

The leader paid him no heed. The hand no longer rested on his head. Shaking, hesitantly, it was sinking inside of it, the fingers disappearing up to the nails.

'Alex, no!' I cried. Out of pure instinct, I tried to run and pull her hand away. Whatever it was that stopped me was as strong as stone, and held me back as effortlessly.

She looked up at me. Her hand had stopped its descent inside the police officer's skull.

'Alex, please, this isn't who you are,' was all I could think to say.

'Don't be an asshole, Charlie,' she said. But still, she released her hand from the officer's head, and turned towards the dark of the alleyway. The flame went out. There was a glimpse of a tail and something gliding above from the streetlamp. And then, with Ghost Frog nowhere to be seen, and Officer Frankopan lying face down on the ground, muttering into the asphalt, they were gone.

***

I didn't give Alex's name to the police when they

arrived. Laura did, along with the names of anyone else we thought we recognised. I'd told my colleague that I wanted a chance to talk to this new street gang leader, see if I could snap her out of it. But Laura said that was Saviour Complex bullshit, and if we didn't tell them who Alex was and what she was capable of immediately, next time she struck it would be on us. Officer Frankopan, although not reduced to a blubbering wreck like Alex's brother had been, was disoriented and upset as he was stretchered away, asking where his wife was and why we were in his house. Still, Laura did not present them with the footage of the incident. Claiming that the situation moved too fast for her to film, she had dropped the camera's memory card inside her high-heeled boot, secreted beneath her heel all the time she talked, safe from confiscation and available for our use. And it was while giving her very detailed witness statement that Laura somehow managed to arrange an impromptu trip to the Facility, the specialised police holding area for problem Stage IIIs.

It was the early hours before the police were finished with us. That didn't matter, though. The Facility was always operational. Situated in a disused warehouse outside the town, I had a feeling of stepping into a Laser Quest venue or a soft play area as we passed through various sets of thick double doors, while the sound of frenetic activity bounced off the walls in the vast space beyond. We would be safe, we were told, as long as we did exactly what we were told.

Once we were finally inside, the impression was compounded, rather than shattered. A fake city street, with buildings several storeys high made from scaffolding and hardboard, lining a roadway that went right to the far end of the room, some way away. No glass in the windows, or lights in the rooms. Old, beat up cars sat in the painted roads, with a surprising number of unlit street-lamps punctuating the sidewalk, only illuminated by a spotlight moon hanging from the rafters. Our guide was Detention Officer McAlpine.

'I can't see anybody,' I said, 'but I can hear them. Where are they?'

'They're in the buildings, somewhere,' she said. 'It's like watching animals in the zoo. Sometimes you've got to wait for them to come out of their house and into the enclosure.'

'How come there are no lights in the buildings or the streetlamps?'

'We cannot risk any of them coming into contact with electrics. Serious potential fire hazard. Similarly, the windows do not have glass in them for obvious reasons. The idea is to provide a safe alternative to the downtown area, where they can let off a bit of steam and satisfy the urges that are particular to their condition.'

There was movement on a higher storey. A figure appeared in a window carrying a large sack over their shoulder. They darted back in again before popping their head out another window. I didn't get a good look at them, but they appeared to be wearing a ridiculous stereotypical robbers' outfit, complete with stripy top and eye mask, while the sack had the word 'SWAG' written across it.

'That's not a Stage III, is it?' I asked.

'No, that's a paid employee of the Facility,' said Officer McAlpine.

'And what are they doing?'

'They are attempting to attract the attention of a Facility user and induce a chase-and-capture situation.'

'Isn't the outfit a little bit obvious?'

'It serves a therapeutic purpose. If we can encourage the Stage III to believe that all criminals look like that, then it will hopefully result in them leaving innocent members of the public alone when released, or if they stumble across an actual crime taking place, fail to recognise it as such.'

'Because the perpetrator is dressed incorrectly.'

'Right.'

The fake criminal popped his head out of the window for a third time. It looked like they were putting less effort into it this time.

'He doesn't seem to be having much luck getting someone's attention,' I said.

'It can take a while. Wait. Hear that?'

There was a thud from the building opposite, as if something had fallen down a full storey. A trundling sound followed.

'Watch this,' said Officer McAlpine. Through the missing door of a fabricated shopfront rolled a

large ball, on top of which sat the torso of a costumed man. It took me a moment to realise that
the ball was part of him, and had replaced his legs.
He did not have much momentum, slowed down
somewhat by his cape. This was getting tangled up
in the ball, threatening to pull him backwards onto
the ground, or worse, strangle him. Every few seconds, he would stop to sort out the cape and try
and get himself started again. Meanwhile, across
the street, the robber waited impatiently, drum-
ming their fingers on the window ledge.

'Come on, Thunderball,' shouted the officer. 'That
thief is gonna get away if you don't catch him!'

Thunderball sighed and pulled his cape out from
under him again.

'I'm on my way, Officer,' he said, visibly frus-
trated. 'I'm on my way.'

'Could we not help him?' I said. 'Maybe give him a
push?'

She shook her head.

'No, they've got to do it themselves, or it just
doesn't register as an achievement for them.'

Just then, there was a blur of movement, and the
robber was somehow not in the window anymore.

'Oh, crap,' said Officer McAlpine. 'She's got him.'

'Who?'

'The Silent Scissor. She's one of the dangerous
ones.'

'Dangerous?'

'Yeah. She's actually quite proficient.'

Suddenly the robber was hanging out a window,

held above the ground by a pair of woman's legs that were clamped tightly round his neck. The woman herself was somehow holding herself aloft by clinging to the window ledge with her arms, her whole body as straight as it could be with a man's head between the thighs. Officer McAlpine approached quickly.

'Officer,' said the masked woman, calmly. 'I caught this man taking something that does not belong to him. He's all yours.'

With that she let go, and the robber fell to the pavement, landing heavily on an already heavily dented car roof. It was only then that I saw he was heavily padded. While Officer McAlpine helped him up, I watched as the woman propelled herself through the air, her legs wrapping round a lamppost for a second before she launched once again and landed on an air conditioning unit on the other side of the street. Dropping to the ground, she disappeared into the darkness, her long legs carrying her silently away at incredible speed.

'I was going to do that, damn it!' said Thunderball, still far away from the scene of the crime.

'I know, I know,' said Officer McAlpine. 'Don't worry. There'll be more criminals to catch in a minute.'

'I guess,' sulked Thunderball, and trundled back the way he came.

'Is he OK?' I said, gesturing to the man in the robber's outfit Officer McAlpine was still supporting.

'Yeah, I'm OK,' he replied. 'Maybe hurt my ankle a

little bit, but I can ride it out.'

'All our actors are trained by Hollywood stunt people,' said Officer McAlpine. 'They know how to fall, take a punch or whatever, without doing too much damage to themselves.'

'Still,' I said, 'it looked quite a drop.'

The robber shrugged. 'They've dropped me from the top floor before.'

'Feel the ground,' said Officer McAlpine.

I did so. It was surprisingly springy.

'They use it in adventure playgrounds,' she said. 'You can fall from way up and not break anything, as long as you're careful.'

As Officer McAlpine helped the robber towards the medical room to get checked out, I looked up the street. Now that my eyes were accustomed to the light levels, I could see that there were conflicts happening right the way up — out of windows, on top of cars, in the middle of the road. I wondered what it would be like to be here all day, in this street of eternal night.

Just then, Thunderball, still trundling slowly back across the road, stopped and looked at me and Laura with suspicion. He paused.

'Look! It's some of King Chameleon's gang! They're in disguise!'

Immediately, heads right down the vast room turned, and feet pounded the hardwood floors inside the buildings. Flying rosies dived down on us, and climbers raced over the rooftops. Fireballs ignited, and eyes lit up with building energy that may or may not have been harmless.

'We have a J Situation,' said Officer McAlpine calmly into her radio, before turning to us with a look of barely concealed panic. 'You need to run. Now!'

We didn't need telling. We were already halfway out the door before the first energy beam blasted a tiny but definite hole in the spot on the floor where we had been standing moments before.

HEROS AND ANTIHEROS

I was talking to Councillor Bob Dash, who sits on the town council of Merriweather, when the call came through. I'd asked him what the financial burden was on a town of this size to have such a high proportion of HEROS diagnoses, and he'd said it was 'an incredible strain', that while they get assistance at both federal and state level, as all hotspots do, ultimately the funding of the extra police and HEROS Support services, not to mention the running of the Facility and Stage IV clean-up operations, meant that the only way to avoid diversions of large amounts from schools, general healthcare and infrastructure was through hefty property tax rises. This issue, he was explaining, now dominated local politics, and was the cause of much frustration to him personally, as a supplementary plan of a 'HEROS tax', payable only by HEROSic people or their primary carer, and designed to take a significant portion of the burden away from the average tax payer, was gaining traction within the council. Although financially illiterate, and doomed to bankrupt every single HEROS case in Merriweather before ultimately collapsing in a series of legal challenges, it was, he was saying, a vote winner. I was going on to ask him if Alex's plan for a downtown HEROS zone was viable, and he was informing me that there was 'not a chance in Hell' of it ever happening, when Laura checked her phone, said we'd got all we needed, thanked the Councillor, and ferried me out of Town Hall before I had a chance to draw my breath.

'What's up?' I said. 'That was bordering on rude.'

'Yeah, well, he was boring,' said Laura. 'This is the good stuff.'

'What is?'

'Bo. He's got a villain.'

***

Bo, or The Trout, danced helplessly at the bottom of the tree in the garden, forlornly letting out his low rumbling noise to no discernible effect on the hairy figure who dangled above from a long monkey-like tail, making 'oo-oo' noises down at him while putting his hands in his armpits. It was awful seeing him reduced to this. A once proud man, now acting out the role of superhero in his front garden like a child, equipped only with a ridiculous costume and a superpower of no discernible use.

'Has he caught him yet?' I asked Paynter, who stood watching anxiously from the kitchen door, sipping on a glass of lemonade. She no longer winced in pain at the noise. She was just used to it, I guess.

'No,' she said. 'Monkey Man... Larry, is really agile. Bo can't keep up, and his power... it just does nothing to Larry. It's like he doesn't even hear it. The HEROS Support worker said in a way that this had happened was a good thing, because at least we know where he is and what he's doing, but...'

Larry the Monkey Man leapt suddenly through the branches of the tree and over Bo's head, landing on the shed roof with a clump. HEROSsories had outdone themselves with his costume. Real monkey fur was finely woven into the Hidron, creating the illusion of natural growth. The cartoon monkey mask, with its big sticky-out ears, was less impressive. Still, I imagined they charged him more than the usual five thousand for it.

Monkey Man shrieked deafeningly from the roof.

'You won't ever defeat me, Trout!' he cried, in a horrible rasp.

'I'll tear down your evil empire if it's the last thing I do, Monkey Man!' Bo shouted back, heroically, his voice muffled by the mask.

'Will you people keep the noise down!' cried a neighbour from an open window across the street. 'I'm trying to watch my shows.'

'Sorry,' shouted back Paynter, shrugging helplessly.

'The noise. The awful headaches,' the neighbour continued. 'It's too much, it really is.'

Paynter shrugged and smiled. After playing out this scenario, over and over again over the past few months, with neighbour after neighbour, and even barely-neighbours from further and further afield as Bo's reach expanded, she knew there was really nothing else to do. The current complainant resignedly huffed and, perhaps sensing the same, disappeared into the dark of their living room.

Meanwhile, Bo continued his melancholy dance, as Monkey Man gave him the finger on both hands above his head.

'It's difficult to watch,' I said.

Paynter nodded.

'I try not to let the kids see it,' she said, 'but it's all the time, nearly. This will still be going on when they get home from school. He just can't leave him alone. I know it's the sickness, but it's… he's got no dignity like this. I'm sorry, I can't…'

I saw that she was crying. She ran inside.

***

'Paynter? Are you OK? Can I get you anything?'

I found her sitting on the living room couch, cuddling her knees as she sobbed. I'd told Laura to wait outside. She said we'd be missing out on a Magic Moment if she did. I agreed with her. I still told her to stay outside.

Paynter looked up at me with her earnest eyes,

red from crying. I saw her head twitch slightly, checking that Laura wasn't lingering in the hall. Then she spoke.

'It hurts, so much...'

I sidled up next to her on the sofa. She seemed so in need of some relief, but I had nothing to offer her. She seemed to have no vices for her to lose herself in, just for a moment. Such was the curse of her wholesomeness. I thought about her living like this for the year or longer it took for Stage III to pass, before... it was too much to even think about. Almost anyone who could afford it would place their loved one in a residential home at this point. For lower income Americans such as Paynter, this was not an option.

'It must be hard for you, to see him so debilitated...' I said, trying hopelessly to put it into words.

She shook her head.

'It's not that,' she said. 'I'm almost used to that by now. It's just... I used to be the most important person in his life. Then the kids came along, and he loved us all the same. Even when he first went Stage III, he'd still be Bo a lot of the time, and he'd express that he loved me then, even though it felt weird. But now, it's all about Larry. It's all he ever thinks about. He only sleeps when he drops down from exhaustion. He's hardly ever Bo, and that's pretty much just so he can have a shower. You know what totally broke me up the other day? It's that bottle of Scotch I got him for his birthday.

It's still half-full. He wasn't a heavy drinker, but he loved his Scotch. And now…. It's like, the man I love, the man I care about, the man I promised to spend the rest of my life with, he's lost interest in being that man. But when he spends all his time at the bottom of that tree, it's like …'

'Does it feel like he's having an affair, almost?' I said.

She nodded, and cried all the more, her head on my chest as I cradled her and sensed that Laura had slipped into the hallway and was filming us anyway. I was glad. It was a good moment, the one that I had needed from her since the beginning. It was true.

***

'Oh, it's you again,' said Dr. Wexler, as a pair of painter/decorators stripped away fire-damaged wallpaper in her near-empty office.

'What happened here?' I asked, looking up at the ceiling that was blackened with smoke.

'Bread machine caught fire,' she muttered. 'Now, what do you want? It's hard enough to work in these conditions without dealing with your constant demands.'

'We were wondering if you could do a quick piece to camera about HEROS villains?'

'You mean Negatives? Fine. Negative Identification is an occasional symptom of—'

'Wait! We haven't started filming yet.'

'Fine. You started now?'

'We'll tell you when.'

'Fine. I'll just stand here, wasting my time.'

'OK, whenever you're ready.'

'You're not going to ask the question?'

'We can dub it in later. Just tell us what Negatives are. In your own time.'

'Fine. Negative Identification is an occasional symptom of Stage III HEROS, in which the sufferer takes on a villainous, rather than a—'

'Sorry, could you do it a bit slower. You sound a bit rushed.'

'I am rushed. I'm very busy. You said in my own time and my own time is fast.'

'Yes, but if you could do again just a bit slower, that would be great.'

'Fine. Negative Identification is an occasional symptom of Stage III HEROS, in which the sufferer takes on a villainous, rather than a heroic alter ego. While many are content to simply torment a Positive nemesis, others actively commit crime, achieving satisfaction from the act in a manner similar to that enjoyed by their Positive counterparts when fighting it. Only when enough crime has been felt to have been committed can they revert to their civilian identity. As is ever the case with HEROS, no one knows why this particular divergence occurs. Is that enough?'

'Yes, very good, but would you mind doing it once more, only this time can you—'

'No. Absolutely not. Get out of my office. They're

measuring for a new carpet and you're in the way.'

***

'Can you use any of that?' I asked Laura, as we drove away, heading for the Bradley River bridge.
  'Oh, I'm using all of it,' she said.

***

Swineboy is a villain. His organ replacement consisting of a slightly pig-like snout for which he has found no use; his villainy mainly consists of littering. We joined him as he scattered the contents of a garbage can in parking lot.
  'Swineboy, why do you do it?' I asked.
  'Whatya mean, why'd I do it? It's a law. You're not meant to drop litter. I hate laws. I love crime. So I'm dropping litter.'
  'Why do you hate laws and love crime?'
  'That's a dumb question. That's like saying why'd ya hate the guy who killed your ma but love your wife. You hate the bad in your life, you love the good in your life.'
  'But killing your ma would be a crime, right? And you love crime.'
  He kicked a can across the lot.
  'Hey, I'd hate that my ma is dead, and I'd hate the man who did it. That's not saying I'd hate the actual criminal act of killing my ma, you get me?'
  'Not really.'

'Anyway, no one's killed my ma, so...'

'Have you ever tried any other crimes, besides littering?'

'Yeah. I mean, I'm pretty limited. I'm not that physically strong. I can't do nothing with my nose...'

'What other crimes have you tried?'

He shrugged. 'Illegal parking. Vandalism. Jaywalking. I'd like to try mail fraud.'

'That's all pretty low-level stuff.'

'Doesn't matter. A crime's a crime. All crimes are equal under the law.'

'They're not, though.'

'I'm talking about the higher law. The law of crime.'

'Is it like a religion for you, almost? Crime?'

'Religion? Nah. Religion's not a crime. They don't pay tax but they never go to jail. What's up with that?'

'No, I mean, the crimes you do don't actually benefit you in any way. In fact, having seen your arrest sheet, you'd be a lot better off if you didn't do crime.'

'Nah, I'd be dead, man,' he said softly. 'Gotta do crime.'

We followed Swineboy out of the parking lot and down towards some lock-up garages.

'This is one of my favourite places to do crime,' he said, taking out a can of spray paint.

'You're going to do some graffiti?' I asked.

'Yeah, watch this.'

On the white door of one of the lockups, he sprayed the words 'I Love Crime'. The 'love' of course represented by a big heart, and signed, or tagged in graffiti parlance, 'Swineboy'.

'You really do love crime, don't you?' I said.

'Yeah, I do.'

'Hey! Put down that can, now!'

A private security guard was approaching us. I had a feeling he might be armed. I was taking no chances.

'Hello,' I was saying to him. 'We're a documentary crew from England. We were just filming a piece with Swineboy here, who has Stage III HEROS, as I'm sure you can tell, and can't be considered responsible for his actions. We'll absolutely pay for any damage caused. We're also very sorry.'

He wasn't even listening, though. He was looking above our heads. There was something on the roof of the garage. It was making him afraid.

I turned. A black shape disappeared from view. I had a strong feeling that there were more people around me than I could see.

'Never mind,' mumbled the guard. 'Just… don't do it again, OK?'

He turned quickly and disappeared. I looked at Laura. She shrugged. Swineboy went back to his tagging. I scanned the area once again. There was no one.

***

Bo caught Monkey Man late that night, a yawning and hazy Paynter would tell Laura in a follow-up call the next morning. Not through the use of his rumble, but simply through sheer patience. The villain fell asleep in the tree, and Bo knocked him down with a stick. He sat on him while Paynter phoned the 'police' or, more accurately, Larry the Monkey Man's wife to come and pick him up.

Announcing that there was still more crime to fight, Bo disappeared into the night, only to climb through his window several minutes later, peel off his costume, and sleep the deepest sleep.

The victory was short-lived, however. Monkey Man was up the tree the next morning, and The Trout stepped out once again to challenge his nemesis.

HEROS IN THE SHADOWS

Me and Laura were taking stock of things back at the hotel. We were due to fly back in a few days. We had more than enough footage for two programmes, full of Magic Moments, an even balance of stuff from the Happy Places and the Dark. With the new footage of Bo we had more than justified the second trip, with us chronicling the progression of his illness from the beginning to near the end. We still had one major piece of filming to do, an interview with popular HEROS performer Spencer Macleavy. The only thing that niggled was our failure to track down Alex. Her story was left dangling, frustratingly unresolvable without her participation.

The police were reluctant to give us any information on the further activities of Alex and her gang, but what we gleaned from Laura's apparently unlimited barrel of sources was that there had been several similar attacks, with police officers attempting to arrest offending Stage IIIs targeted. The gang was apparently growing steadily, with eyewitness reports of anything up to twenty black-clad rosies appearing out of the shadows. Many of Alex's friends — Janvier the sparker, Marian with the tail, Raymond the glider and more — had disappeared with her.

Whether any of the officers suffered the same damage as Officer Frankopan, now thankfully out of hospital and recuperating at home, with only a few days of his memory missing, was something no one would confirm. All that was known was that the gang would vanish in the manner that they came, often taking the offending Stage III with them. Sometimes these would reappear after a couple of days in a safe location, evidently fed and looked after. Others, often those living in precarious or impoverished circumstances, would never be seen again.

'We can't just give up on this,' I told Laura. 'Viewers are going to want to know what happened. They're following a story arc and then they just zoom off the top or something.'

'I agree, it is unsatisfactory,' she said. 'But *no one* is spilling. Everyone we know is in the gang has vanished, and as for everyone else, either they don't know how to get to Alex, or they're so totally sold on what she's doing, they're not going to risk it for anything, least of all our dumb TV show.'

'Maybe they're just scared she'll put her hand in them and fry their brains?' I said.

'I don't think so,' said Laura. 'I've been doing this long enough to know fear from loyalty. These people are not afraid. In fact, since the Eraser has come along, everyone on the street is less afraid. She's giving them hope.'

The Eraser. Why did she have to have called herself that? I wanted to ask her, and was annoyed that I couldn't.

'Have you tried her parents again?'

'Yes, and guess what? They really don't want to speak to us.'

'Not like you to give up so easily.'

'Hey, I'm ruthless. I'm not a prick.'

'What if we asked them to their face?'

Laura's mouth dropped open in mock-horror.

'You want to doorstep them?' she said. 'Wow. Think I just saw your principles fly out the window, Chas.'

'No, not doorstep them. Just, maybe, I dunno, happen to bump into them somewhere. Cross paths, totally coincidentally, and have a chat while we're there.'

Laura sighed.

'I'll see what I can do,' she said.

***

And that was how, after some sterling but ethically questionable detective work from Laura, I found myself standing in front of Michael and Kathryn Felton as they examined vibrating pillow cushions in a Walmart on the good side of Merri-weather.

I looked up from the beanbag I was pretending to be fascinated by.

'Hello! Mr and Mrs Felton, isn't it?' I said, in my best surprised voice. 'I was just looking at bean-bags.'

'We don't really want to talk to you, if that's OK,' muttered Alex's dad.

'I quite understand,' I said. 'After what happened to Jim. How is he, by the way?'

Michael looked torn between sticking to his guns about not talking to me and addressing a polite en-quiry into the well-being of his son.

'Well, he's…'

'He's doing as well as can be expected,' his wife answered for him.

'Of course,' I said. 'And how well is that, if you don't mind me asking?'

Alex's dad frowned, annoyed enough to engage with me now. 'Alex did something to his mind, young man. He is missing a large number of his memories from the past ten years. He's very con-fused and often upset.'

'I am so sorry to hear that.'

'So if you see our daughter on your travels, tell her… just tell her…'

'Not to call,' said his wife, holding back a sob.

'Do you know where she is?' I asked.

'No, of course we don't know where she is,' said her dad. 'Now, if you'll excuse us. And don't bother us again.'

With that, they walked away.

I absentmindedly fondled a vibrating neck cushion as Laura appeared from the corner she was hiding round.

'They don't know where she is,' I said. 'And she's done a lot of damage to Jim. And I'm guessing to those police officers too. You're right. She's actually really dangerous.'

'Yeah,' said Laura.

'I still like her though,' I said.

***

It was the next day. I'd pretty much given up on seeing Alex again. Maybe it was best that I didn't. She'd obviously gone somewhere quite extreme, and I doubted I would be able to remain objective. So all that was left to do now was interview the legendary Spencer Macleavy, get the tiny snippet of concert footage his people were allowing us to film, have a celebratory burger, and fly home. Me and Laura were in Starbucks, prepping for the interview, when I felt a hand on my shoulder.

'Hey, Charlie! You're still here!'

I looked round. It was Kenzie. No longer wearing camo, her small wings peeking out from behind a large rucksack.

'Kenzie!' I cried. 'You got out of Rosetown!'

'Yeah,' she said. 'It was getting kinda nuts up there, what with the discipline and the guns, and there was some attempted coup against Steve, I think over the food. It failed, but I thought, somebody's going to get shot real soon, so I hit the road and hitchhiked my way back here.'

'So what's the plan?' I asked, after persuading her to sit with us a minute. 'Are you back in Merriweather for good?'

'No, I'm just touching base with a few people. I'm actually going to stay with my sister in New York for a bit.'

'Really?'

'Yeah. I'm just… how can I put this? I'm tired of everything being about rosies, you know? Rosie rights, rosie zones, rosie towns, rosie menace, rosie… whatever. I just want to stop thinking about it for a bit. Maybe think about me as a person, who happens to be a rosie. Stop being a soldier in a war that maybe only other people want. Maybe I'm being selfish but…'

'Not at all. You've got to look after yourself.'

'So what are up to?' she asked.

'We're just here for one last day of filming and then we fly back late tomorrow. We're going to be interviewing Spencer Macleavy, believe it or not.'

'Oh my god, I love him. Are you going to the concert?'

'Yeah, we're going to be side of the stage actually.'

'I am so jealous,' she said, clutching her chest. 'I mean, obviously he's a role model, but I love the music as well. Anyway, I gotta go. My train leaves this afternoon and I still got a mountain of stuff to do.'

'Well, Kenzie,' I said, as we hugged, 'it's been really great getting to know you and talk to you for the programme, and I wish you the best of luck in all that you do... You heard from Alex recently?'

She sighed in resignation at the inevitable question.

'No, not since Rosetown. You?'

'I met her in an alleyway,' I said. 'She was melting a police officer's brain at the time. It didn't look like she and her friends wanted to talk.'

'Yeah, I heard about that,' she said, sadly. 'I think that's the kind of thing I'm trying to get away from.'

'I suppose I just want to speak with her, give her the opportunity to explain why she's doing what she's doing.'

'I wish I could help you,' she said. 'But I got a train to catch, so...'

'No, problem, Kenzie,' I said, and waved her on her way.

***

I expected Kenzie was telling the truth about Alex. By the sound of it, they weren't on the same page anymore, so an easy dialogue between the two of them seemed unlikely. Still, it was only a couple of hours after that conversation, while I sat alone in the car, waiting for Laura to ostensibly shoot some establishing shots of the highway, but really to take an urgent-sounding phone call she didn't want me to hear, that the passenger door of the car opened, and Alex, hidden away inside a black hoodie, sat behind me.

'Hi, Charlie,' she said, spreading herself across the seat.

'How you doing, Alex?' I said, trying to not sound as pleased to see her as I was.

'I'm OK. I'm good, actually. Better than ever.'

'Not wearing your costume?' I said.

'I'm not at work.'

'And what is your work now?'

'Freeing my rosie brothers and sisters from the tyranny of a police state.'

'That's quite a step up from the Rosie Zone.'

'People change and move on, Charlie. They grow.'

'Yeah, you've moved on, Alex. Not sure you've grown. Prepare to be erased? What's that corny bullshit?'

'It's catchy. It communicates. It'll sound good on your show. That's the point. You said I had a knack for that, remember?'

'You certainly have that. Which raises the question, why have you turned to violence instead of using your impressive communication skills to improve conditions for rosies peacefully?'

Alex shook her head with disbelief.

'Listen, you psychopath,' she said. 'I know you followed me to Rosetown. Stalking me, yeah, cute. But one thing I realised there with all the bad camo and awful food, was that there's no such thing as

Stage Is, Stage II, Stage IIIs, whatever. Together, we're HEROS. We're all one thing. Those rosies out there the cops are whaling on all the time, they're my family, way more than my mom and dad and Jim and whoever. And if someone was carting members of your family off in a paddy wagon and making them run around some sick maze, wouldn't you just stop them? By force, if necessary?'

'I guess, I—'

'You hear about the butcher? I know you interviewed him. Police got tipped off he was showing his customers a costume and they took him out with a tranquiliser dart and took him away. You think anyone's going to see him again?'

I was shocked to hear that news about Wayne. But the idea of using something like that as justification for what happened to Officer Frankopan did not sit well with me.

'I would hope his family got to see him again,' I said, 'but you can see the police's perspective, can't you? He could be very dangerous, with that blade.'

'So could any physiotypical who owns a knife, but you don't see them rounded up and taken away in the night.'

'But you're doing a lot of harm with your power, Alex. Your parents say Jim is in a bad way, and that police officer... Are there more like him?'

'It was just a mistake with Jim,' she muttered. 'Don't you think I feel bad about that, like, every day? Anyway, I know what I'm doing now. We're all getting to know our replacement organs better. That cop, he's fine. And he'd probably be even more fine if you hadn't messed with me while I was doing it and made me shaky. But I needed to send a message, make them afraid. You think I wanted to do it? It wasn't fun for me. I did it because it was necessary.'

'Necessary? How can you say that?'

'Because I haven't had to do it again. Now the cops just run when they see me. But that's all done, anyway. We're moving to a new phase of operations now.'

'And what's that?'

'You'll know when you see it. Anyway, you're talking to my parents now, asshole?'

'You're a hard person to find.'

'Hey, I posed for your stupid camera down that alley, what more do you want? And you giving names to the cops? Real dick move.'

'You couldn't seriously think we wouldn't.'

'I did, actually. I trusted you not to.'

'Sorry to disappoint you.'

'It's OK. Not many people meet my standards.'

'How many are in your gang now?'

Alex shrugged.

'Thirty, more. And we're not a gang. We're a community. If a rosie we find on the street is in a bad way, we look after them.'

'Where's your hideout?'

'Up your ass.'

'Very good,' I said, trying not to laugh. 'The question is, is it the Batcave up my ass, or a supervillain's lair?'

'What do you expect me to say? Boring question.'

'Did you make the costumes?' I said.

'Yeah, pretty much. Need a bit of help sometimes. But I can stay solid and do them nearly all myself now, if I concentrate.'

'You did a good job. I really liked them. Lots better than HEROSsories.'

'Thanks,' she said. For a second, she looked genuinely touched. 'Listen, I got to go.'

'I'm flying out tomorrow,' I said. 'So I probably won't see you again. But thank you for letting us get to know you, Alex. It's been an experience.'

'Bye, Charlie,' she said, and slid out the car door.

Laura waited a minute for Alex to disappear out of sight before joining me.

'You'd better tell me you had your radio mic switched on just then,' she said.

'I did. You get any visual?'

'No, I was standing there with the lens cap on. Of course I did. You think she knew we were filming?'

'Yes. No. Maybe.'

I smiled for a second. We'd got what we needed, just about. An end of sorts. But I felt like I'd just said goodbye to a friend.

HEROS ON SHOW

'Hey, I know you! I watch your shows on YouTube! Charlie, right? I thought I knew the name. You're the guy who talks to all those crazies who believe in aliens and do weird sex shit dressed as dinosaurs and stuff.'

'Yeah, that's me. The younger me anyway.'

Spencer Macleavy gave me a hug. We were backstage in his dressing room, his PA out of shot as we filmed him preparing for his big show. Up until now this had mostly involved him drinking curious liquids and gargling while wearing a Pikachu onesie. After several minutes of this, he had finally clocked who I was.

'I cannot believe it's you!' he said, the hug going on longer than an Englishman can generally handle. It wasn't so surprising I should be recognised like this. While other documentary filmmakers had their back catalogue available on paid streaming services, the channel didn't even care enough about mine to bother having my old stuff taken down when uploaded illegally to YouTube. My Sneering Years had a long afterlife for which I wasn't even paid.

Spencer Macleavy, on the other hand, looked like he was doing rather well for himself. His tour bus was a long, silver expensive thing squatted out the back of the casino venue. His watch cost more than my fee for the programme. Although very much a marginal figure in the music world as a whole, amongst rosies he was perhaps the biggest star of all. His incessant touring took him from hotspot to hotspot across the world, playing mid-sized, out-of-the-way venues to packed houses of fans, with only the occasional venture in to large cities.

'Is it OK if we do a sit-down interview now?' said Laura, probably in an attempt to end the hug as much as anything else.

Spencer glanced at his PA who nodded, holding up five fingers.

'Five minutes,' she said. 'Spencer needs to rest his voice before the show.'

With puppy dog enthusiasm, he settled himself upright in a chair by the dressing table, on which sat several rows of neatly arranged Star Wars toys. I wondered if these were part of his rider.

'What do you want to know? You can ask me anything.'

'You can't ask him anything,' said the PA. 'I mean, use your common sense, OK?'

I asked him when his organ replacement took place ('six years ago, when I was eighteen'), if he had been musical before it happened ('not at all, I was completely tone deaf. I'd clear the room at karaoke, ha ha!'), and who his greatest influences were ('Justin B, Justin T, Tina Turner and Sinatra'), while he picked up the Star Wars toys and punctuated his answers with play battles. Then I asked him how he felt about being an icon, even a role model for rosies the world over.

He put the toys down and looked appropriately solemn.

'Obviously, it's something I take very seriously,' he said. 'I feel honoured, and humbled, and proud to have a position in the hearts of so many of my rosie brothers and sisters. And because of that, I take care not to let them down. I hope you will never see me behave in a way that would bring the rosie community into disrepute. God, it would be awful if anyone ever felt I had breached that trust.'

I asked him where he stood on issues of rosie rights, social integration, and separatism.

'Oh, I don't do politics,' he said, smiling. 'But I have love for everybody.'

And does he consider Sympathetic HEROS to be HEROS?

'I have love for everybody!'

***

Out in the concert hall were many familiar faces. There were the gladiators, Don The Pummellor and Third-Eye Slim, sat together in their civvies with both their families. Don spotted us and gave us a friendly wave with one of his enormous hands. Pummelling was not on his mind tonight.

Also, there was little Lizabeth, out with Mom and Dad and not wearing any kind of helmet, her tusks getting no attention from anybody.

'Oh, she just loves Spencer,' said her mom, Jenny. 'Always sings his songs around the house. This is like a dream come true for her.'

'What's your favourite Spencer song?' I asked.

'Whatever You Are is Beautiful!' she cried, excitedly, and sang a few bars. I wondered if I'd ever seen a child so happy.

Next we ran into Hope and Lorne. Hope dragged her whip behind her proudly, and was sporting a new catsuit, cream and studded with rhinestones.

'The other one is just daywear,' she said. 'This is for special occasions.'

'Do you feel you fit in with this crowd?' I asked.

'Absolutely!' she said. 'Why wouldn't I?'

'And you haven't felt any hostility from anyone?'

'No. I don't feel any hostility here. I actually don't feel it anywhere now, in the rosie community. I guess people are realising what unites us is more important than what sets us apart.'

Indeed, dotted about the concert hall were various people like Hope, with synthetic replacement organs, some in costume, others not.

Also to be found, dressed in their regular camo, were two rows of residents of Rosetown, including, surprisingly, their leader, Steve.

'Didn't have you down as a Spencer fan,' I said as we passed.

'The boy is a beacon,' he said. 'I am working towards converting him to the separatist cause. With him onboard, it will only be a matter of time before we have a full HEROS state to ourselves.'

'How are you trying to convert him?'

'I send him letters via his management.'

'Have you had any response?'

'Not as yet, but it's early days.'

'How long have you been doing it?'

'About two years.'

'Is that really early days, Steve?'

'When you've been waiting for freedom as long as I have, everything's early days.'

I was still more surprised to see Gina, Alex's ex, somehow sitting cross-legged on a fold-up seat. She claimed she had no interest in Spencer or his music in itself, but was here to show support as an ally.

'What do you make of the Spencer phenomenon?' I asked.

'Well, look around you,' she said. 'Is this not a prime example of what Foucault called heterotopia? A liminal space, where established social order is suspended, making room for a series of critical reversals and subversions, allowing interrogation of normative practice to take place. Now, if we were to factor in one of the conclusions reached by Deleuze and Guattari in their analysis of Kafka...'

I left her to it.

Sat near the front was Brett and Abbie ('I suppose I should feel sorry for the people behind me, but I don't!'), and Landon Starflower ('I'm gonna light up for Spencer brighter than I ever lit up for anybody, and that's the truth!'). In her own box, legs stretched out and wearing her usual velour tracksuit, sat Phoebe, all by herself, pouring popcorn onto her writhing tentacle tongue, enjoying the best seat in the house.

I wondered who else might be found here, if I searched hard enough, amongst the costumed and un-costumed figures? Theo the Rippler perhaps, or maybe even some of the Stage IIIs monitored by Officer Frankopan, if any of them had the level of support needed. The only people I knew who would definitely not be there would be Alex and her people. And Bo and Paynter, obviously. Bo would almost certainly be circling his tree right now, while Monkey Man mocked him from above.

What was striking looking at this colourful audience, with all the outfits, appendages and growths, was that no one looked the odd person out. They all belonged here, whatever was going on with their body, and however they chose to present themselves. The most startling group of people in the world, and they weren't even looking at each other. They were staring at the stage, waiting for Spencer, the most precious rosie of them all.

***

The five-minute bell rang, and we hurried backstage to get in position to film the tiny amount of material we were allowed to without paying a substantial fee to Spencer's publishing company. Watching from the side we could see his backing band take their positions, still shielded from the audience behind a curtain. Eventually, Spencer appeared, still swigging his unusual mixture, and nodding at various female backing singers and percussionists. Taking his mark, he glanced up at the stage set as if for the first time, a little boy lost in a dreamland.

'Cool,' he said, to no one.

There was a signal to begin. The drummer counted them off, and the curtains parted. The audience went wild. Winged rosies flew above their seats, eye beams shone in delight, and sparkers sent up jets of flame that threatened to set off the sprinklers. And this was all before Spencer had even begun to sing.

Like Bo, Spencer's organ replacement involved his vocal cords. Unlike Bo, he could do something useful with them. Spencer could mimic any sound. He could be any instrument, he could have any voice. He was a human synthesiser, his only limit being the sounds in existence for him to copy. He had no voice he could call his own. Instead, he would drift during the course of the song from Bieber to George Michael to Snoop Dogg to Beyoncé. He took his own instrumental solos, perfectly recreating the sound of a piano or a distorted guitar or a violin. Even at one point, a whole band of bagpipers. I thought his music was gimmicky and pointless. What was the point of singing with the timbre of Tony Bennett without the life experience to back it up? But Spencer's audience heard it in an entirely different way. To them, every note was a moment of triumph, a rosie setting their sights on the best the physiotypical world had achieved, and matching it. *We can do this*, his music said to them. *We are as good as they are.*

We got the footage we were allowed, twenty seconds of 'Whatever You Are Is Beautiful'.

'Do you want to watch this?' asked Laura.

I shook my head.

'Let's get a drink,' she said.

***

We were sat at one of the bars in the casino complex.

Laura's phone buzzed with messages.

'You're very popular,' I said.

She grimaced. 'I might as well tell you,' she said. 'My son, Lukas. You know he's been living with his dad, right?'

I nodded. That was about all I did know.

'Yeah, well. There's been a pretty major falling-out between them. He's being doing some drugs. Nothing serious. Just weed. And pills. And acid.

OK, relatively serious. Anyway, the upshot of it is they are no longer on speaking terms and he wants to come and live with me for a while.'

'And that's a problem because…'

'Because I'm not in the country for weeks at a time. You're not the only globe-trotting documentarian whose arse I wipe. If he moves back in, I can't work. Which is fine, but you know that with half these guys, if you let them down once, you don't get a second chance. So I'm trying to get him talking again with the dad, who thinks I'm soft on the whole drugs thing because of my dissolute lifestyle or some crap… Anyway, it's a mess.'

Laura ordered another round of drinks.

'Hey, you're the designated driver, remember?' I said.

'Fuck it,' she said. 'We'll get an Uber. Or maybe just stay here until one of us is sober enough to drive.'

And so over the next couple of hours, knocking back exactly double the amount of booze as me, Laura told me all the stuff she had been keeping to herself all the years I knew her. Open relationships, closed ones, marriage proposals, failed pregnancies. True love, dependence, betrayal, heartbreak. A whole emotional life, recounted sardonically at one remove, punctuated by messages from home and frantically typed replies. Sometimes I thought I saw a rawness poking through, and maybe even the first beginning of a tear.

It just about felt like it was all winding down, and

I could relax my 'good listener' face, when I heard someone call my name.

'Yo! Charlie! Over here!'

It was Spencer, calling us from inside a roped-off booth the other side of the bar area. We must have been there longer than I thought, so engrossed in Laura's tales I hadn't seen his arrival. Now the concert had finished, the audience gone home, and Spencer was out celebrating with an entourage of physiotypical-looking men, who could have been friends but looked like security, and five women, some of whom were definitely rosies and others may have been.

I nodded politely, but didn't want to engage. This was time I was giving Laura, time I owed her after all the years of her making me look at least competent.

Spencer beckoned. 'Come over here, man! I want to talk to you.'

I ambled over, careful to not look too eager for his company.

'Hi. Great show, by the way.'

'Did you stay for it?' he said, eating the praise as if he wasn't expecting it. 'Did you really think it was good?'

'Yeah. It was really great.'

'What was the best song, do you think?'

'Um… Whatever You Are is Beautiful.'

'Yeah. Everyone likes that one. It probably is the best. Listen, I don't want to talk about me. I want to talk about you! In fact, what I would really like to do is have you accompany me and my friends here to my hotel suite and talk us through all your old shows. I'm dying for these guys to see them, especially these ladies here. We'll play them on the big screen. It'll be like our own private cinema.'

'Listen,' I said, not able to think of anything worse. 'I'd love to, but I'm just giving some time to my friend here. She's having a rough time of it and…'

'Hey! She's more than welcome. I mean, doesn't she help you make the shows?'

'She's my director, yeah. And camera, and sound. Everything, really.'

'So the two of you, come up to the suite and tell us about these crazy films you guys made! You gotta, Charlie, please? It'll be so dope.'

'I'll see,' I said, and sauntered back to Laura, hoping she could come up with a good reason for us not to.

She looked up from her phone and smiled at the suggestion. 'Yeah, why not?' she said. 'Let's do a retrospective. Fifteen years of fuck-ups from Laura and Chas.'

I realised she was very drunk. If I'd ever seen her this drunk before, she'd held it together a lot better than she was doing now. Whatever was happening on her phone was not good for her equilibrium.

'We don't have to,' I said.

'Oh, Chas, we do have to. Listen, I want to see that I've done something right, OK?'

I glanced at Spencer. I should have said no. Called

a taxi. I guess I just wanted to make Laura happy somehow. I gave him a thumbs-up.

***

'Dude, how do you just stand there while that guy's nailing his dick to a bench? I'd be like, stop doing that, bro!'

'I… I just had a job to do and… you get used to the craziness after a while.'

'Oh, my god, it's gone right through. The nail has gone right through!'

Up in one of the several bedrooms in the hotel suite that Spencer apparently needed, my greatest hits played out in front of me to high shrieks and low bellows of disbelief from the mass of bodies sprawled over the bed, across chairs, rugs and laps. We'd done UFO spotting, ghost hunting, extreme eating, cartoon character orgies and bodily mutilation. The onscreen me had sneered through every minute. The offscreen me had tried to drown his shame in champagne while crouched on the floor. Laura was slumped over her phone in the corner, a bottle to herself, oblivious to anything going on in the room, her desire to go over our past triumphs evaporating with the first text message she got after stepping in the room. I felt stupid for bringing us up here.

'Look, it's been great,' I said, when the episode finally ended. 'But we need to go. Our flight's tomorrow. We've got a lot of stuff to sort out…'

'Bullshit,' cried Spencer from the bed, between two rosies, one covered in tortoiseshell cat fur, the other sporting a fine peacock's tail. 'We haven't watched my favourite episode yet.'

'What one's that?' I asked.

'This one.'

He queued up another video on his tablet. I knew from the first shot on the TV screen which one it was. It was my first rosie film, from years ago. Forty-five minutes of me making fun of them, dressing up in costumes and pointing out their differences for laughs. I felt the ground open up beneath me.

'Do you really want to watch this?' I said.

'Sure? Why not? It's the best one.'

'Well, don't you find it offensive?'

'No! Why? It's great! It's like, you're saying, hey, rosies, I've been having a great time with all these UFO nuts and ghostbusters. Now it's your turn to come to Charlie's party.'

I didn't understand. All this time I'd been beating myself up over these films, and the very people I'd presumed would be upset couldn't even see the problem? It's not as if the sneer wasn't there on the tape. I knew it was, because I put it there, and I could see it played back now. Maybe Spencer and his crew couldn't read it for what it was. Perhaps my sneer was drained of meaning once it crossed the Atlantic.

Meanwhile, on the screen I was roaring like a bear at a man's claws.

Laura's phone rang and she staggered up.

'I gotta take this,' she slurred, and tried to open the door one-handed for some time. One of Spencer's people eventually held it open for her, and she disappeared into the corridor, calling somebody, her ex or her son, a shit and a prick, before the door shut with a clunk, seemingly wiping her voice, and any trace of her, from the sealed existence of the suite.

The episode continued. I was wearing a cape, a big letter C on my chest and my underpants outside my trousers. Spencer and his entourage roared with laughter as I lay on top of a car pretending to fly while interviewing a wobbly glider. I didn't know what to think anymore. Were they wrong, not to be offended? Was that even possible? I didn't like the person on the screen, but what if I had just internalised the criticisms of a prissy UK press? Was old Charlie actually... OK?

My head was swimmy from booze now, time slipping away from me as I sat. The rest of the programme happened without me noticing it much. I wasn't even thinking about how long Laura had been gone. Suddenly the programme was over, and Spencer was sliding off the bed, his two girlfriends in tow. His male friends were already holding a door open for them, the girls from their laps still clinging to them.

'Hey, Charlie,' he was saying. 'Me and the girls and the guys are just going to go into the other bedrooms for a while. But, hey, you can stay here, relax, and Felicity here will keep you company.'

I looked behind me. One of the girls who may or may not have been a rosie was lying on the bed, staring blankly at the screensaver on the TV.

'I've left something for you in the bathroom, and,' he said, leaning in and whispering, 'you see that girl with the tailfeathers? They're *coming* out of her asshole. I'm gonna stick my dick right in the middle of them!' He giggled like a schoolboy. Then he was gone, along with the rest of them.

Felicity on the bed said nothing. Already I'd forgotten what Spencer had said about a gift in the bathroom. Then I remembered, and stumbled over to see what it was.

Laid out on the toilet seat, along with a tightly-rolled $100 bill, the most beautiful line of coke. I had never seen one neater or straighter.

I should have closed the door and walked away, gone and looked for Laura. But after all that booze, the only thought that was in my head, one that alleviated years of guilt and somehow gave me permission for anything, was, *old Charlie is OK after all*. And old Charlie took charlie, and that was why I was kneeling down and sniffing the toilet.

***

I fell out of the bathroom, grinning like an idiot, that good old dry feeling at the back of my throat. The past few years of my life swiftly evaporating. Sam a flicker of a thought, too indistinct to signify anything past the raw fact of her existence, and that wasn't nearly enough to do any good now. Everything that Charlie did was good and whatever Charlie wants he should have. Even the stuff he doesn't want, he should have, just in case he changes his mind.

There was a naked girl on the bed.

Naked! the dumbest part of my brain shouted. That means sex. Sex with someone who might be a rosie. You wanted to have sex with a rosie, remember? Find out if she's a rosie and if she is, fuck her. And if she's not, fuck her anyway.

'Are you a rosie?' I said, unzipping my trousers and lowering them to my ankles, because that is what you do when you are Charlie and you've taken coke and there is a naked girl in the room, even if you're so far from horny it's untrue.

'Yeah, I guess,' she said, still staring at the screensaver on the TV.

'What do you... what do you do?'

She rolled her eyes.

'You really wanna see?'

'Yeah,' I said, nodding eagerly.

'This,' she said, and a wave passed over her entire body, leaving it a perfectly reflective mirror. And in its distorted contours I saw myself, eyes wide, teeth bared, as much of an erection that the alcohol would allow popping out of the fly of my boxers, about to cheat on the woman I loved simply because the opportunity presented itself. I had never seen anything so monstrous.

'I… I gotta go,' I said, hurriedly poking my deflating penis away and pulling my jeans back up.

'Why?' she said, seemingly annoyed at the rejection of the sex she didn't want to have. 'You got a problem fucking a rosie?'

'No!' I said. 'I *really* want to fuck a rosie. Well, I thought I did. But actually, I don't. I don't know what I want. I mean, you, you're beautiful. Not to objectify you. But I would, if I… But I can't.'

'Whatever,' she said, reaching for the TV control, as I headed for the door.

'I'm really sorry,' I said.

'Your TV show was offensive bullshit, you know that?' she shouted after me, just before the door closed on her and the brightness of the hotel corridor burned my eyes.

HEROS IN ABSENTIA

I lurched down the corridor, looking for some way down and out. The euphoria from the cocaine had turned into a parody of itself, a sickening rush that just wouldn't stop. Laura had called me several times, but I had been too drunk to notice the silent mode vibration. I managed to focus on my phone long enough to get it to call her back. It went straight to answerphone.

And somehow I was in a lift. Somehow I was in the casino, looking for Laura between the rows of slot machines. Laura wouldn't be here, I must have thought. She might be at the bar. There were so many bars, it seemed, but no Laura. I might have been circling the same bar. I couldn't tell anymore. I was going to fall over if I didn't sit down. There was a long seat in a dining area, closed for the night now. I'm not sure what I had to step over to get to it, but I was there, and I was not asleep, but perhaps not awake either as I spun round and round while lying perfectly still for what seemed like a year.

And then I was awake. A cleaner was prodding me with a litter picker.

'You can't sleep here, sir,' they were saying.

It was morning. I knew that not because I saw sunlight. They don't have windows in the casino, so you lose all track of time. I knew it was morning because I could smell the heavenly aroma of American coffee.

***

I tried to buy a cup using the $100 bill I found in my pocket. They let me have it for free. Once I had established my stomach was probably going to accept it, and remembering the quest for Laura I'd been on before I had to lie down, I said goodbye to my new friends in the food court. I tried her phone again. Still the answer message. The car. If I could find the car in the parking garage, then I would be one step closer to finding Laura. I headed unsteadily in that direction, coffee in hand.

A drip of coffee had just escaped the plastic lid, scalding my fingers, when I saw a familiar face, stepping out of a lift. It was one of the girls from the night before, the one with tortoiseshell cat fur. She had more clothes on now, quite elegant in fact, as she walked primly across the foyer, a Hermès handbag swinging at her waist. She pretended not to see me.

'Hi! Excuse me! Miss!' I called out to her, almost

running.

'Oh. Hi,' she said, looking in the opposite direction.

'Yeah. I won't bother you for long. I just need to know, have you seen the friend I was with last night. Laura. The one who got up to make a phone call and didn't come back.'

She looked blankly for a moment.

'Oh, her,' she said, finally. 'She seemed really negative. No, we didn't want her back in.'

'What? What did you mean?' I said.

'What I said. Now stop bothering me. I gotta go.'

And with that, she walked away, and threw the revolving doors into what might have been sunlight.

***

Of course, the parking garage was huge, I had no memory of what storey we were parked on, or what the car number plate was. I wasn't even sure of the make of the car. I knew that it was red. After exploring several identical looking floors, and realising that the coffee wasn't going to stay down after all and stopping to be sick in a disabled bay, I collapsed in a corner, defeated.

I don't know how long I was there for. I was feeling so ill, being curled up in the corner of a concrete multi-storey car park wasn't without appeal. But I knew I couldn't stay there, and I was achieving nothing at the complex. I made my way down to the taxi rank, hoping that the $100 coke-caked bill would cover the considerable ride back to Merriweather.

***

It only really hit me when I was in the back of the cab, avoiding the driver's attempts at conversation about sports I didn't understand while swallowing my sick, how badly I'd screwed up. I'd taken cocaine again, after all this time. Would this kickstart cravings again, once I'd overcome the desire to vomit everywhere for all eternity? I shuddered at the thought of feeling better and finding out. But that was nothing. I'd nearly cheated on Sam. Although we'd never explicitly stated we were in a monogamous relationship, we obviously were. I couldn't claim innocence. No, I'd come perilously close to smashing the most important relationship in my life apart with a sledgehammer just because I got drunk and because I was drunk I took coke and because I took coke I thought I was God for five minutes. I felt sick, not just with alcohol, but with myself. The idea of going back to the hotel, finding Laura, and having to talk about the night before, suddenly seemed unbearable. But the thought of only having something as repellent as myself for company was even worse.

We weren't far now. The Bradley River Bridge was in sight.

'I've changed my mind,' I said to the driver. 'I

want to go somewhere else.'

***

I can't explain why I asked the taxi driver to take me to that house, out there on the outskirts of Mer-riweather. Maybe I just needed to feel something that was pure and good. The lawn grass. The smell of their breakfast. The big white fridge. It wasn't professional, turning up unannounced with sick on my breath in clothes I had slept in. It wasn't even rational. Perhaps in hindsight I could explain it away as something of a stress reaction. Or maybe I just don't get to rationalise it.

The tree was free of Monkey Man when I got there, and Bo was nowhere in sight. When I rang the doorbell the house was quiet. No kids running or demanding food. The curtains were drawn. Through the glass pane, I saw no signs of life. The taxi had already gone, leaving me stranded in this suburban neighbourhood where the roads don't even have pavements. I really hadn't thought this through. I rang again, in blind hope.

Footsteps, on the stairs. Unsteady, unrhythmic. A figure moving in the hall. The door opened. It was Paynter, in a bathrobe, her uncombed straw-berry blonde hair exploding in many directions, a big plastic cup of lemonade and something spill-ing over her hand. She was very drunk.

'Schaaad… Hi!' she slurred.

'I've come at a bad time,' was all I could think to

say.

Not. At. All. You've come at the *best* time. Come in. In. In. Now. In.'

She beckoned me inside. I stepped into the darkness.

'It's quiet,' I said, stepping over something broken on the floor. 'Where is everybody?'

'The kids are with… their friends.'

'Like a sleepover?'

'Yeah. Yeah. A sleepover. But longer.'

'And Bo?'

'Bo? Oh, Bo's out looking for crime. Bo's *always* out looking for crime.'

'What about Monkey Man?'

'Monkey Man… moved on, Chad. Come. Come this way. Come into the parlour.'

'Said the spider to the fly?'

'Say what?'

'Never mind,' I said, following her into the living room. It smelt a lot of booze and pizza and slightly of sick, more so than me. There was a fair bit of the latter on the floor. It had been less than a week since I had been here, but things had deteriorated fast.

'Sit. Sit here,' she said, collapsing onto the sofa, and patting a tiny space left at the end.

'I could sit on a chair,' I said.

'No. Sit here. Next to me. Sit.'

I gingerly sat down. Now that I was there, I was thinking of how I could leave.

Paynter stood up. 'You don't have a drink. I'll get

you a drink!'

'No, it's OK,' I said. 'It's a bit early for me.'

'Well, I want a drink.'

'You look like you already have one.'

'I want more a drink.'

She disappeared into the kitchen. I heard sloshing. I thought about slipping out the door right then, but it didn't seem right just to leave her like this.

Paynter returned, her large cup filled to the top.

'It's a drink I invented myself. It's called… lemonade and gin.'

'Ah, ingenious. I didn't think you drank.'

'I don't! Well, right now I'm drinking. But I don't. I don't like the taste. But the other day, Bo was climbing down his tree and nearly dying, the kids were just going on and on at me about something I don't even remember what and I just thought, I need something. Something to make this not what it is, which is Hell. And I saw the bottle of Scotch. The one I bought for his birthday. The one that he'd never even finished because he was the Trout now, and the Trout don't drink. And I poured myself a glass. And I added like, a ton of water. And I drank it. Like, gulp. And I nearly threw up. But I didn't. Not that time. But I nearly did and I thought boy, that was a mistake. I ain't never doing that again. But you know what? A few minutes later, for the first time in forever, I wasn't thinking about Bo falling out of the tree. I wasn't thinking about the shitload of money I've had to pay to people five fucking miles away whose trout have died and somehow that's my fault. I wasn't thinking about anything much except my head was tingly and I wanted to laugh. And I thought, you know what? I'm going to have another one, and I did. And then I've had another one and another one and the liquor cabinet's nearly empty and I hate it and I feel like throwing up and sometimes I do throw up but by god I love the not thinking!'

'I understand,' was all I could think to say.

'So, tell me, Chad,' she said, sidling up to me again, 'is there a Mrs. Chad back home, Chaaad?'

'Um, yes. I have a partner, Sam. We've been together several years.'

'Oh, that is so sweet. I think everyone should be like you. Everybody should have somebody for… love and stuff.'

'You have a partner. You have your husband, Bo.'

She put her face too close to mine and looked at me as if she was examining a pet. She seemed so far from the girl with the earnest eyes I had been introduced to just a few months ago. Had the experience of looking after Bo changed her so utterly? Or was I simply seeing a side to her she had no reason to reveal to a visiting documentary crew from England, now revealed to me through the psychological stripping of alcohol? It hit me hard that, outside her role as Bo's wife and carer, I had no meaningful idea of who she was at all. I really wasn't that good a journalist.

'Do you know something, Chad?' she was saying.

'Bo is a horny guy. I mean, like, really. I mean, I like sex, but he *likes* it likes it, if you know what I mean. He used to want it, like, all the time. Even when the kids came along, and I was *soooo* tired, he'd just want it. But since the HEROS and The Trout stuff… he's not even interested. He won't come near me! It's like The Trout takes all his sex energy.'

'That's sad,' I said, as she rested her head on my shoulder and I felt her hand on my chest. I noticed she needed a shower.

'We haven't done it in months, me and Bo,' she sighed. 'I never thought I'd miss it. But Jesus fuck, Chad, I miss it.'

She stood up suddenly.

'I want music!' she cried. She pulled her phone from between two cushions. 'Listen to this!' she said. Some modern country music with a patriotic theme. It was loud. It was horrible. 'Isn't it great?'

I smiled non-committedly.

She danced to the music, provocatively swinging her hips as the country singer pledged to honour the troops.

'Dance with me!' she cried over the music that somehow managed to be deafening despite coming out of a tiny speaker.

'I don't dance really…'

'Come on, Chaaad, dance!'

She shimmied over until she was inches away. I jiggled from foot to foot politely, as only an Englishman can. I could feel her against me now. I stepped back, but trying not to cause offence, not so far back it looked like I'd stepped back. I probably should have stepped back farther because then her arms were round my neck and she was kissing me enthusiastically, her tongue in my mouth and her alcohol-soaked breath in my throat.

I gently pushed her back, but she didn't take the hint. Instead, her arms got ever tighter, to the point I was being gently strangled, and her tongue felt more and more like a foreign body invading me.

And that was when Bo said, 'Hi, Chad.'

STAGE IV

HEROS IN CRISIS

Bo had been wearing sweatpants, a t-shirt and his crocs when he had walked downstairs, the sound of his recent entry through the window and quick shower presumably drowned out by the overwhelming tinny noise coming from Paynter's phone.

When he came down again, after silently turning and going the way he came, however, he was dressed as The Trout. This time, he did not acknowledge me. He did not acknowledge his wife, shocked by his presence into something vaguely near sobriety. Instead, he walked purposefully past us, as if going to work, his expression a mystery kept behind his mask, and headed out the front door. And it was from the front door we watched him dumbly as he got in the 4x4 he was no longer allowed to use, drove away, taking a muffled rumble and a stabbing pain behind the eyes with him.

'Oh, that's bad,' said Paynter, as he disappeared round the bend.

'What do you mean?' I said.

'HEROS Support said, if he's Bo, he's OK. If he's The Trout, that's OK. But if he's The Trout and he does Bo things… Oh, god!'

She sobbed uncontrollably into my shirt.

***

After making sure HEROS Support were on their way, I tried Laura again. She picked up and for a second I thought there might be a god after all.

'Laura, I can't believe I've found you. Where have you been? What happened to you last night?'

'I couldn't get back in the room. Those rosies had put up one of their psychic barriers. Guess they didn't care for me.'

'One of them did say you seemed negative.'

'Like I haven't heard that before. Anyway, I tried to call you, you weren't picking up, so I slept in the car, then drove back to the hotel. But Chas, where the hell are you?'

'I'm at Paynter's and Bo's. Ah, it's quite serious. Thing is, Bo's gone Stage IV.'

'Oh, shit,' she said. 'That's really bad. Are you sure? I thought that wouldn't happen for ages?'

'The HEROS Support guy said normally it takes a year or more, but it can be triggered by a sudden shock.'

'Has he had one?'

'Oh yeah. Thing is, I think it might be partially, slightly, my fault. I've, ah, I've really messed up, Laura.'

'I'm coming to pick you up,' she sighed.

***

I couldn't stop looking at Paynter on the drive with the HEROS Support team as we took off. I felt like I was leaving the scene of a crime. She was in good hands, better and more useful than mine. An all-points bulletin had been sent out for Bo's car. But still, I felt that seeing as I'd broken it, somehow I should fix it. Laura had no intention of letting me stay, however.

'What were you even doing there, Chas?' she scolded, as the house disappeared out of sight.

'I just… I did something stupid. Well, several stupid things, one after another, after you'd gone. First, I took some coke…'

'Oh, Chas.'

'And then… I nearly cheated on Sam with one of the rosie girls.'

'Chas!'

'You see, I've… I've been struggling with a thing. An urge to have sex, with a rosie. I mean, I thought it had gone, and it had, for weeks, but in the moment, it came back. I don't know why it was even in my head. I mean, I'm not into freaky stuff, normally, and I'm happier than I've ever been with Sam… I just don't understand it, Laura.'

Laura took a deep breath.

'Two words, Charlie. Midlife crisis. Sure, you're happy, but you're stuck. You know what your future is. You'll stay with Sam, having the same unimaginative sex you've always had, and just before her biological clock runs down too far, you'll give into pressure and have a kid. It's a 100% dead cert, and it's coming towards you like a bullet. But buried in the back of your mind is old Charlie, and he's jumping up and down, saying, hey, I'm not dead yet! Get me out and let's have some fun while we can! It's your last gasp of youth, shouting don't box me in, don't define me as this boring guy in a sensible relationship who will be a dad and be good at being a dad and then slowly grow old and quietly die. Well, newsflash, Charlie. You are old. You're bald, and I stick a filter on everything to make you look better. It's too late, Charlie. You'll never learn that fourth sexual position. The only thing left to do is be contented and happy.'

I sat in stunned silence.

'That was a very strange mixture of comfort and devastation,' I said, finally.

'No problem,' said Laura. 'So carry on with your story. How come you got from one inappropriate situation with a woman to another?'

'I... I just needed to be with someone. Talk to them. And you weren't there, and it wouldn't have been right with you anyway because you know Sam, a little bit, and...' I trailed off in despair at myself.

Laura shook her head.

'Chas, Chas,' she said. 'Always looking for a mummy to look after him.'

It stung because it was exactly true. I suddenly

saw myself as Thunderball back in the Facility, a silly creature caught in a series of pointless, repetitive self-defeating behaviours. Except I was worse than Thunderball, because I could see my many capes were bad ideas, doomed to get tangled up beneath me and pull me backwards, but I still ended up wearing all of them.

'And then?' Laura asked, dragging my mind back to the car.

'Then I turned up at their house. And Bo wasn't there, and the kids were somewhere else, and she was there, and she was drunk. I mean, really drunk...'

'Yeah, I could see that coming. Well, either that or meth amphetamine. But then what happened? No, let me guess. She came onto you and...'

'She kissed me. I didn't kiss her back. And Bo had come in through the window, had a shower, changed, come downstairs...'

'And saw you. Jesus.'

'And he became The Trout again and went out the front door instead of the window and drove off in his car. Which is really bad.'

'It is bad,' said Laura. 'Really, seriously bad.'

'It's the worst there is.'

'For them. And it's pretty bad for us, too.'

'We don't matter right now! How can you even think about that? Actually, how is it bad for us, exactly?'

Laura sighed. 'It could be very bad for the programme. I don't know if the programme can even be a thing after this. I don't even know if *you* can be a thing after this.'

I gulped. 'I don't understand.'

'You kidding me? You can't see it? You fly out to make a sensitive, heartfelt doc about HEROS, and while you're here, you kiss the wife of one of the subjects of the programme and send him into Stage IV? If a word of this gets out, you're gone. For good. In every way.'

I stared at the road ahead. In a moment of heavy silence, I saw my own life, and Sam's, and Laura's, and Paynter's, and Bo's, all tied up in a web of my own ineptitude. My motives for saying what I said next were a perfect balance of noble altruism, protection of those I cared for most, and shameless self-preservation.

'We're going to sort this,' I said.

'You can't sort Stage IV HEROS,' said Laura.

'I know. But let's sort this anyway.'

***

'Dr. Wexler, could we have a minute of your time? I just need to ask — it's incredibly bright in here.'

I shielded my eyes from the vivid new paint scheme of Dr. Wexler's office.

'Yes, I happen to like pink and yellow. They're my favourite colours. What of it?'

'Oh, nothing. Just the combination is… intense. But we can work around that. I just need to ask you about Stage IV…'

Dr. Wexler sighed.

'Do you need me to do something to camera? I'll speak as slowly as I can but I have a dental appointment in two hours.'

'No, I just want you to tell me. If someone has Stage IV, what can you do to calm them down and get them back to a manageable state?'

Dr. Wexler looked at me with disbelief.

'Get them back? You can't get them back. Once they go Stage IV, that's it. Endgame.'

'Come on, Dr. Wexler, there must have been some case where it's at least been postponed, or—'

'Young man, when a HEROS patient becomes a Stage IV, they have entered a trancelike state where internally they can no longer separate their civilian identity with their crimefighting alter ego. Inevitably, their inability to house two separate personalities in their mind will cause catastrophic mental distress, despite their apparent outward calm. Without fail, the Stage IV sufferer will, within twelve to twenty-four hours, be overtaken with the thought that the only way of relieving this distress is by taking permanent action.'

'They will want to kill themselves...'

'They will need to. Their belief in this course of action will take over their mind absolutely. They will not be dissuaded. They cannot even hear you if you attempt to do so. They will apply any and every available method to achieve their own death, drawing on reserves of strength and ingenuity they may never have possessed before. They will try, and if they do not succeed, they will try again, and again, until finally they achieve their aim.'

'But surely there are ways of restraining them...'

'Then they will bite through their own limbs to free themselves of any restraints. True, you could put them in a padded cell and a straitjacket, but they can then never leave that room or take the straitjacket off. So the question is, do you wish to see all Stage IVs contained like that for the rest of their natural lives, or do you let their illness take its natural course?'

I sighed. I was getting nowhere with her.

'Dr. Wexler, you know the rosie situation here better than anybody. Where do Stage IVs end up going to do it?'

'Do you want a map?'

'Have you got a map?'

'Of course.'

'Yes. I want a map.'

Dr. Wexler handed me a photocopied laminated map of Merriweather, numbered and annotated with details of top rosie suicide spots.

'Thank you,' I said.

'Bring it back when you're finished. It's laminated.'

***

We drove. Over the Bradley River Bridge. Down to the reservoir. To the top of every parking garage in Merriweather. And we walked, into the heart of the most secluded woodland, along the marshy banks of the Bradley River. We climbed up the highest of towers and rockfaces. Everywhere in Merriweather and the surrounding area where rosies had been known to go to take their own lives, we went. But we found no sign of Bo, or the car, or heard a solitary low rumble in the distance.

I had wanted to keep on going well into the night. Laura had to make me stop at various points during the day, just to drink some water and eat. But it was now nine o'clock in the evening. We should have been on a flight home by now. We had been going for nearly twelve hours. And Laura said that if I wanted to keep going, I could, but she could do no more. And she was right. Neither of us could. We had been to everywhere marked on the map, and various places that weren't. Several times we had passed police cars, no doubt also on the lookout for Bo. Wherever Bo was, it seemed, it was a place we would not be able to find him. A garage lockup, perhaps, or an empty building he had broken into. Good intentions and willpower were not enough after all. I had failed.

The weight of my own uselessness crushed down on my shoulders as we drove back to the hotel, rain miserably beginning to fall. I checked in with HEROS Support. Paynter was under sedation. There were no leads. Bo was already dead somewhere, I knew it. I tried telling myself that it was the illness that had killed him, not me, but I didn't believe it. And selfishly, stupidly, I realised that the chain of events that led to Bo's death would inevitably come out, and I would never work again, and Sam would go. It would just be me, my memories, and a coke habit to keep me company, I thought, as we crossed back over the Bradley River Bridge. That was my future now. Coming towards me like a bullet.

So it was something of an upswing in my fortunes then, that Laura said what she did.

'Hey! There he is!'

Standing by the barrier on the side of the bridge in the rain, looking down into the gushing water below, was The Trout.

Perhaps he sensed he had been spotted, because it was then that he rumbled, sounding deeper than ever before, ominous in its tone, like the cry of some lost deep sea creature, and for the first time, continuous. If it was meant to keep people away, then for the first time, it seemed, Bo had actually found a practical use for his headache-inducing power. We watched drivers swerve as they tried to deal with the sudden jabbing pain they felt inside their skulls, we knew that we could not be dissuaded. It wasn't just Bo's life that was on the line now.

By the time Laura had found a place to dump the car and we'd scrambled back down the pedestrian walkway, a car driven by an elderly driver had already crossed lanes and narrowly missed being ploughed into by a container truck in front of our very eyes as the rumble kept going for an unfathomable seventh minute. It was hard to walk towards him. The temptation to turn, and distance ourselves from the rumble's radius of influence, was strong. But the need to try and fix my mess before someone died because of my uselessness was stronger.

The Trout was no longer standing by the barrier. Instead, he was sitting on it precariously, the glassy eyes of his costume gazing into nothingness, while his human eyes stared into the water below through tiny holes in the mask. While he attracted the attention of the few rubberneckers who could bear the pain, there was no sign of the help we had already demanded. There was meant to be a safety net lining both sides of the bridge to catch any leaping Stage IVs, but below Bo, a hole had been burned, presumably by a jumping rosie with the ability to do such a thing, and had yet to be repaired. All he had to do was push himself off, and he would be swallowed by the water below.

'Bo!' I cried helplessly, and probably a bit too loud for dealing with someone who could fall to their death at any time, as I edged nearer and nearer to the centre of the sonic assault, my head feeling like it was leisurely being sliced in two.

'Bo, listen to me! You've got to stop the noise. Someone's going to crash. People are going to die! Please, stop it, Bo!'

The trout head did not move. I did not know if it even heard me. I wondered if I should just grab him, or better yet, get Laura to put the camera down for a moment and grab him with me. But it would take just the slightest awareness of what we were about to do, or just the sheer wetness of rain-drenched rail, to send him plummeting.

The rumble stopped. The immediate feeling of relief was the sweetest thing I had ever felt. Maybe he would have stopped it eventually anyway. It must have been exhausting keeping it up for that long. Or maybe I'd proved the good doctor wrong, and I could get through to Bo on some level, even when he was as far gone as this. All I could do was carry on, barely giving me a moment to absorb the fact I might have just saved some lives, which was definitely a plus in my favour on the cosmic scales.

'Listen,' I babbled, pathetically unable to find the calming tone and pace necessary for the situation, 'there's nothing between Paynter and me. What you saw, was just a… a mistake that was made because Paynter loves you so much and misses you. I wouldn't make a move on your wife, Bo. Firstly, I respect you too much, and secondly, I'm very much in love with my partner. And actually, I've had this weird thing going on recently where I've been finding myself sexually attracted to rosies, so I wouldn't have even be thinking about your wife in that way anyway. So what I'm basically saying is, there's nothing going on and please don't jump.'

The head still did not move. But the legs did. Still holding on to the rail, he pushed himself that bit further forward, as if carrying out a trial for his actual jump. I looked at Laura. She shook her head from the other side of the camera I realised now she was simply hiding behind, terrified by her own impotence.

Bo pushed himself out with his legs again, a bit further this time. We'd only been there a little more than a minute, but it felt like an eternity. An eternity that would end very soon, and very suddenly, before help could arrive.

And then, I saw and understood what I must do.

I began to pull myself up on the barrier, next to Bo.

'Chas, no!' cried Laura.

'It's OK,' I said, unconvincingly.

It took me longer than I thought it would to get my legs over, using muscles I hadn't used for a while, but there I was, sat next to The Trout, holding on to the rail just as he was, my bare hands already cold and wet without the protection of Hidron. All it would take for me to fall would be to let go.

Still, that trout head did not move.

'I want to jump, Bo,' I said. 'If I did, would somebody save me? Are there any superheroes in the area? Like The Trout, for instance?'

'Get down!' shouted Laura, behind me.

The Trout said nothing. His head did not turn.

'I mean, if I were to drop right now, I don't think I'd survive the fall. I really would need someone to do something heroic and save me now if I was going to survive.'

Still, nothing.

'Chas, if you die on me now, I swear I'll kill you!' screamed Laura.

'I'm going to count to three, and then I'm going to jump,' I said, not really knowing where I was going with this. 'One.'

No movement from The Trout. Hysterical crying from Laura.

'Two.'

Was there something just then? A slight turning of the neck? Perhaps it was just an involuntary movement. There was nothing else.

I waited for some reaction. A sense that he saw value in my life, and by extension of his attempting to save it, his own. But it was not forthcoming. My heart beating sickeningly fast, I said what I had set myself up to say.

'Three.'

At this, his head turned. And I felt my wet hands slipping on the rail, and I was falling, falling to the water below, with no one reaching out to save me.

HEROS IN EXCELSIS

I'd misjudged the situation completely, of course. Bo, like all rosies who had reached Stage III and beyond, had no interest in doing good. They were not superheroes. They were crimefighters. They fought crime compulsively, simply because crime existed, not because to do so was right. Bo only acknowledged me at all, just before I fell, because he was probably trying to figure out if committing suicide was technically a crime.

Nevertheless, in my first moments of falling, I felt a strange acceptance of my own imminent death, as if everything was how it was always going to be, and I had merely played my part in some great cosmic drama. This acceptance disappeared very quickly, however, and I screamed in terror as the air cut my face, my eyes shut tight to hide the freezing, rushing water I was about to hit at great speed.

And then something hit me, at a greater speed, it felt like, than I was falling. Except I wasn't falling anymore. I was... flying?

I had no choice but to open my eyes. Something black, wrapped around me. And above it, what looked incredibly like a small, fleshy wing, gliding a moment, then turning in the air at great speed, becoming a blur that strobed the lights on the bridge above. All the while, a clapping sound I could not place battered my eardrums.

'Kenzie?' my muffled voice said, my mouth pressed against a shoulder.

'Incoming!' Kenzie shrieked, and then we were not flying but landing, quite painfully, cutting through the reeds that lined the side of the riverbank before finally coming to rest in the thick mud that passed for dry land there, a few feet away from a row of very solid-looking trees.

'Ow,' I said, weakly, knowing I was quite cut up but too grateful to be saved to wanting to be seen making a fuss about it.

'Yeah, I can't really do landings yet,' said Kenzie, letting go of me and raising herself up. I couldn't see her face. It was covered by the full mask that was part of the uniform of Alex's gang.

'Never made it to New York then,' I croaked, as I felt myself slipping further into the mud.

'I guess not,' she said.

'How come you can fly now?'

'Me and Alex worked it out a while back. I'd always thought my wings should work like a bird's because of how they look. But they're more like an insect's. Clap them together and make a vortex. I rise up to fill it. It's obvious when you think about it.'

'It so is.'

'Charlie, you asshole!'

A voice called to me from the thick riverbank foliage. I was in no state to stand up, so could only lie there and wait for Alex to arrive and abuse me further. And sure enough, there she was, towering over me, in full Eraser gear.

'We had one flyer ready to catch that rosie, and we wasted it on you. What were you thinking?'

'I just thought that maybe, if he had to save me, like he was a superhero…' I could see the contempt on Alex's face, even underneath her mask. 'Oh, never mind.'

'You've been snooping around in our lives for months now, and you still understand literally nothing. We should have let you drop.'

'You're all heart, Alex,' I said.

'He's going to go!' someone shouted. I realised that there were more people around me. Perhaps quite a few people more. Their forms took shape as my eyes adjusted to the darkness. Alex's gang, and there were more of them than ever.

I pulled myself up, and followed Alex and Kenzie's gaze.

'Shit! They're not ready!' cried Alex, as a speck of a figure dropped from the side of the illuminated bridge, disappearing into the darkness beneath.

'They've launched!' someone shouted.

From another point in the bridge, something else

dropped. I could not make out the shape, but it was too big to be one person. And it was not falling. It was gliding. Gliding towards a point in the air where Bo would very soon pass.

Whatever it was, it was not fast enough. Bo plummeted though that space, just as whatever it was approached. There was a cracking sound that reverberated off the metal of the bridge struts and into the night. A second later, and Bo hit the water.

There was one last ineffectual rumble, smothered by the river. A slight pain at the back of my skull. A lone trout landed suddenly on the mud and flapped helplessly. I waited for more. A whole shoal to pay final tribute to Bo. But there was nothing more.

'He's gone under!'

'No, I see him!' said another rosie, whose telescopic eyes bulged out of his mask. 'But he's caught in the current. He'll be gone in seconds.'

'They can get him if they do another sweep,' said Alex. 'We need light!'

And there was light. An intense glow saturated the river, its point of origin somewhere behind me. I turned around, but had to shield my eyes from its incredible luminescence. Still, I could just about make out the outline of a figure. This rosie did not wear the uniform that Alex provided. They had their own one, in the brightest colours.

'Starflower?' I said.

'The one and the only,' he said. 'Here to save the day in the most spectacular style!'

Alex was less optimistic.

'He's probably gone already. You realise we could have saved that rosie if it hadn't been for you, Charlie? Kenzie was ready to catch him but you had to go first. We got a back-up team, but a glider can't launch or manoeuvre like a flyer can, so Kenzie was really our one shot. Thanks, Charlie. For everything.'

I waited for her to call me an asshole. That she didn't was even more damning. I stood up and threw the trout back. It was something, at least. In that moment, I remembered how all that time ago, Alex had said if I had HEROS, I'd be The Super-Absorber, how I lived on the pain of everyone I talked to for my programmes. I wished I was The Super-Absorber now, and could swallow up the river, draining it, leaving Bo to sink harmlessly to the bottom of the riverbed.

'They can see him! They're going for it!'

Whatever or whoever it was still in the sky swooped under the bridge. Two people, it seemed. One rosie flying, or at least gliding, using their underarm webbing. Attached to them by some sort of harness was a second, dangling something down towards the river. A rope, it looked like, but this glinted, metallically. That cracking sound again, and the rope was now pulled straight, attached to something in the water.

'They got him!' shouted the bulge-eyed man.

'Go! Go! Go!' cried Alex, and her entire gang abandoned me, right there on that muddy bank, as they ran as one towards the river. The reeds seemed to know they were coming, and flattened themselves down as they stepped over them, and into the water.

They would drown, for sure, I thought. But there was no water for them to drown in. It pulled back as they advanced, almost as if some force was repelling it. At once, I could see what they were doing. The natural force field that arises when rosies are gathered together, they were using it as a bubble, keeping them safe and dry. The river passed harmlessly beneath their feet, as they moved towards Bo and his airborne rescuers.

In the far distance, I could see the rosies pull Bo into their protective shell, and those who had saved him from the current descended and joined them. They turned and headed back towards me, Starflower's light extinguished now the rescue was over.

'Well, Charlie, he's alive,' said Alex, as they returned, two of the biggest rosies holding him up. His Trout mask discarded, Bo was unconscious but breathing, his drooping moustache framing a wide open mouth. I had no idea what broken parts his costume was holding together, however. It was a good chance, I thought, that it was that very costume from HEROSsories, made from highly protective Hidron, that had saved his life.

'You need to get him to a hospital,' I said.

'I know that, asshole,' she said. 'But... we just need to do one thing.'

The rosies placed him down on the mud, keeping his head upright. Alex sat down next to him. She took her glove off.

'Alex, you can't!' I cried.

'Watch, and learn,' she said.

Her hand slipped inside his head. I thought about wrenching it out, but knew even attempting it would only bring down the wrath of many rosies upon me. So I stood and watched, as Alex appeared to rummage around in his skull, turning her hand this way and that, frowning with concentration, before smiling with satisfaction and withdrawing.

'His wife will like him more now,' she said.

Bo's eyes opened. He blinked several times. He looked around at the masked faces in the moonlight. He settled on the one person not wearing one. Me.

'Chad?' he said, his voice a whisper.

'Yes, Bo, it's Chad,' I said, bending down and squeezing his hand. 'You've had a fall. We're getting you to a hospital.'

Bo looked down at his silvery costume.

'What am I wearing?' he said. 'Where are my shorts, my crocs? I remember now. I was talking to you. You had that lady with the camera with you. I played football with Mason in the yard. You filmed that. And that was... that must have been yesterday. What am I doing here? Are you people rosies?'

I looked at Alex.

'What have you done?' I asked. 'Have you... fixed him?'

She shrugged. 'Probably not for good. But I've taking him back to Stage I. He'll have to go through all the stages again before he's Stage IV.'

'But, Alex, this is incredible! When did you work out you could do this?'

'I dunno. Yesterday. The day before. I forget.'

'You can't keep this to yourself! You've got to share this with the world.'

'Yeah, love the sentiment, but small problem. I'm on the run for melting the mind of a police officer. Kinda like not being in prison for the rest of my life, you get me?'

I considered for a moment. Two things collided in my brain pleasingly.

'I might have a solution,' I said.

Meanwhile, I looked around in search of Bo's rescue team. One was clearly Raymond, the glider. He gave me a friendly nod. But who was the other? I didn't recognise her at first, without the catsuit. But the glint of the whip coiled up on her belt gave the game away.

'Hope?'

'You betcha, Charlie!' she said, winking from deep within her facemask.

'I guess you've softened your stance on Sympathetics, Alex,' I said.

'I just needed someone with a whip,' she muttered.

'That's the closest you'll get to her admitting she was wrong,' said Hope.

'Not wrong. Just practical.'

The sound of helicopters in the distance cut through the air.

'We need to go,' said Alex. 'You know what, Charlie? You could actually be useful. Stay here with Bo. Jump up and down and get their attention. He'll probably get to hospital a lot quicker that way.'

'But I need to talk to you,' I said. 'How can I find you?'

'Send up the Bat Signal,' she replied, and followed the other rosies into the blackness beyond the trees.

***

'Dr. Wexler! Dr. Wexler!' I cried, banging on the door of her surgery, in the early hours of the morning.

'Are you sure she even lives here?' said Laura, yawning. 'She probably has a flat somewhere else.'

After being reunited at the hospital, where Laura, fresh from filming the entire rescue from up on the bridge, had tearfully informed me that while climbing onto the barrier was the dumbest thing she'd ever seen anyone ever do in her life, she was very much glad I wasn't dead. We'd then spent some time giving yet more witness statements to the police, with a great emphasis from myself on Alex's gangs being heroes, which they really didn't want to hear. For once, Laura was ready for bed while, though delirious with tiredness, I still wasn't done.

A light came on. The door opened. Dr. Wexler stared her Basilisk stare at us from the doorway.

'What can you possibly want now?' she said. 'And why are you covered in mud. Actually, don't tell me. I'm not interested.'

'What would you say if I knew a way you could cure HEROS, Stages II to IV? Well, not cure, but, what's the word, negate? Send back to Stage I, just keep doing that every time they get it, so it never makes it to the end?'

'I'd say, you're not expressing yourself very well.'

'But, hypothetically, would you collaborate with a wanted dangerous criminal, if you could do that? End the late stages of HEROS? Just have Stage I, which is, you know, the fun stage. Well, not fun, but...'

'You're babbling. But in answer to your question, yes. Yes, I would.'

For a second, I wanted to kiss her. I did not kiss her.

'Then, Dr. Wexler,' I said, 'I think we might have the perfect solution to all our problems.'

'If this has anything to do with the unusual reports I received about a patient at the hospital this evening, then that is... satisfactory,' she said. 'Perhaps you can tell your hypothetical dangerous friend to visit me at the surgery, if they happen to be real. Now, please, let me sleep. And go home back to England. You've been filming here for months. There's nothing left to film. Please, go.'

She closed the door in my face. I whooped with

joy.

HEROS UNDONE

I helped Paynter get Bo in his wheelchair up the ramp and through the front door, while Laura, naturally, filmed the whole thing.

'Surprise!' cried all the friends and neighbours who hadn't helped Paynter at all, as we wheeled him into the living room where a banner read 'WELCOME HOME BO' and balloons bobbed about. The kids, back from their extended sleepovers, let off poppers, and showered Bo in hugs.

'Let's not forget the hero of the hour!' said Bo, pointing in my direction with a showbiz flourish. 'This guy — you're not going to believe this — jumped in the water *himself* to save me, then talked all those other rosies into dragging me out and after that, they were gone, and he was the one who waited with me until the helicopter came. How about a hand for Chad?'

'Well, it wasn't quite like…'

My sentence was cut off by applause. Applause I didn't feel I fully deserved, but maybe did, a little bit. Alex could have been right about me. I may have been The Super-Absorber who fed off people's pain, but I might have left a situation in a better shape than I found it, for once. But the golden rule of reporting is to not make yourself the story, or so I was told by a proper journalist who was explaining to me why I was shit at an awards ceremony afterparty once, and so I deflected by simply saying, 'This is Bo's day, it's all about Bo.' Paynter had provided everyone with a glass of champagne, and a shout of 'To Bo!' settled the attention back where it needed to be.

'Look,' said Paynter, showing me her glass. 'I'm drinking fizzy water.'

'You not drinking anymore?' I asked.

'Oh, I'm not drinking *ever* again,' she said. 'And Chad… Charlie, I just want to say I'm sorry about what happened. I put you in an awkward position.'

'No, I'm sorry. I shouldn't have been here. I was just… dealing with my own stuff and I made a bad choice.'

'Well,' she said, 'our bad choices got us to this. So were they really so bad?'

'Now there's a question to keep you up at night,' I said.

She smiled, sensing the moment for a parting of the ways had arrived.

'So… thank you, for all that you did, I mean, at the bridge,' she said. 'And if you see your friend with the magic hand, thank them from me, OK? From us.'

'I will,' I said, and smiled, and got ready to leave.

***

I was sat in the airport café, texting an impatient Sam our ETA. She had been frantic for me to come home ever since she found out about the river incident. I'd explained we still needed a few wrap-up shots. She'd replied she didn't care what we needed, she just needed me back home with her. But now, here we were, nearly ready to go. All I had to do was sit and wait for Laura to win an argument about the dimensions of her hand luggage. Actually, there was one other thing. As I drank the American coffee for the last time and inhaled the aroma of pancakes, things I had a hunch I'd be craving a lot more than cocaine for the next few weeks, a short figure swallowed by their black hoodie slid into the seat opposite me.

'Hi Alex,' I said. 'So you got the Bat Signal.'

'Well, here I am,' she said.

'Can you wait for Laura to get back here, so we can film you one last time?'

She shook her head.

'I am in and out of here. Film me on your phone or you don't get me at all.'

'Fair enough. What's going on with you, Alex?'

'Same old. The community's getting bigger. We're going to need a bigger hideout. The police are still after me. I'm risking everything to be here, just so you know.'

'I appreciate it, really.'

'I should think so.'

'And you've connected with Dr. Wexler?'

'Yeah. Kinda. Turns out you can't just go round doing new medical procedures. You gotta do clinical trials, see if it's just me or all sandhands who can do it, what the side effects are, make sure no one drops dead ten days later yada yada, like you Gen Xers used to say. Anyway, Doctor Wexler's trying to work a local politician, some guy you spoke to…'

'Councillor Dash.'

'Yeah, she's gonna try and get something going that keeps me out of jail if I can help her. I mean, I'll believe *that* when I see it…'

'I hear Officer Frankopan's doing OK. Maybe it won't be so bad for you.'

'You're so naïve, Charlie. You don't mess with cops and get an easy ride. But Dr. Wexler's a good person for trying. I mean, she could go to jail too, just for helping me.'

'Yeah, she is. Has she given you any of her French bread?'

'Not yet,' she said, smiling a rare smile. 'I'm working on it. Listen, I gotta go.'

'Well, I guess this is goodbye then,' I said, genuinely sad to see her really, properly go from my life. I reached over the table to hug her. I was surprised by how enthusiastically it was returned.

'Bye, Charlie,' she said. 'And you're not an asshole, OK?'

'Don't ever say that.'

***

We were airborne. In the seat next to me, Laura was going over the latest footage on her laptop, the plane trip providing her with a welcome break from the texting to and fro. I felt bad for her. Her crisis carried on with no end in sight. As her headphones blared, I heard my own voice explain to Bo on the bridge how his wife meant nothing to me, and I was actually struggling with an impulse to have sex with rosies.

Laura caught me looking.

'Oh, don't worry,' she shouted to the whole plane, over the sound of her headphones, 'I won't use this bit.'

I gestured for her to take the headphones off.

'Maybe we should,' I said, quietly. I'd been thinking about this for the past few days, waiting for Bo to come home and to get that last bit of footage. About the programme. About more than the programme. 'I mean, it's part of the story we're trying to tell, isn't it? Can we really leave this out?'

Laura looked at me with disbelief.

'Are you crazy?' she said. 'OK, two things. Firstly, Paynter and Bo don't need your honest filmmaking shit screwing up their lives, and secondly, neither do you. You've got a good thing going with Sam. Don't drive a bulldozer through it just because of some aesthetic doctrine you subscribe to. Seriously, Chas, don't be a prick.'

'Maybe I should tell her anyway,' I said, my voice sinking into a mumble. 'Maybe not about Paynter, but about the rosie in the hotel. Everything that's good in my life happened because I started telling the truth. About myself, about the people in the programmes. I just want to be able to live with Sam forever and be happy, but I don't know if I can if I'm carrying a secret around with me all the time. The truth is better than a lie, isn't it? I mean, isn't that something that's pretty established?'

Laura patted me on the shoulder.

'Chas, here's the thing. If you tell her, she will forgive you. Women like her, women like me. We always do. We forgive the dumb thing our manbaby did, and we carry on forgiving him, until he does something so stupid we finally wise up and stop. But however much we forgive, the things that are done always leave a mark. They stain. Every text I get from my ex right now, I see the stain on it. Nobody wants total honesty. Nobody can handle it. That's why we edit, filter, so they don't see the stains. You don't need to show the stain, Chas, not one that small. It's just masochism. Self-indulgent bullshit. Go live your life. Be happy.'

***

I collected my bags off the carousel and headed for the arrivals lounge. When Sam saw me, she cried my name, and she ran. She wrapped her arms around me, and covered my face in tears and kisses.

'Don't ever go away again!' she said.

'I won't!' I said, and I was crying too. I wasn't sure what I meant, but I knew that it was true.

BOOKS BY THIS AUTHOR

Hound Dog

Flying Saucer Rock & Roll

The Shuffle

Erotic Nightmares

Whatever You Are Is Beautiful

Printed in Great Britain
by Amazon